CRUM

Mike Kiger
— March 04 —

Vandalia Press publishes fiction and non-fiction of interest to the general reader concerning Appalachia and, more specifically, West Virginia. See our website at vandaliapress.com to learn of forthcoming titles.

CRUM

Lee Maynard

With an introduction by
Meredith Sue Willis

Vandalia Press

Morgantown 2001

This novel is a work of fiction. Names, characters, places and incidents are either the product of the author's imagination or are used fictitiously. Any resemblance to actual events or locales or persons, living or dead, is entirely coincidental.

Vandalia Press, Morgantown 26506
© 2001 by West Virginia University Press

All rights reserved

First edition published 1988 by Washington Square Press. Second edition 2001

Printed in the United States of America

10 09 08 07 06 05 04   10 9 8 7 6 5 4 3 2

ISBN 0-937058-59-9

Library of Congress Cataloging-in-Publication Data

Maynard, Lee 1936 -
    Crum/Lee Maynard —2nd ed. with an introduction
       by Meredith Sue Willis
    192 p. 20 cm.

PS3563.A96384 2001   2001093428
                                       CIP

Vandalia Press is an imprint of West Virginia University Press

Book design by Alcorn Publication Design

Cover photo by Lyntha Scott Eiler, CRF-LE-C116-02
Courtesy of the American Folklife Center, Library of Congress

Printed in USA

This book is dedicated
to
Amos and Minnie Maynard

CONTENTS

An Introduction to *Crum* by Lee Maynard

By Meredith Sue Willis

Each time I read Lee Maynard's *Crum*, I ask myself why this foul-mouthed, sexist, scatological, hillbilly-stereotyping novel is one of my all-time favorites. On the surface it is simply the story of a boy's last year in his hometown, filled with humorous and crude events. It is divided into sections named after the seasons, and it pretty much follows seasonal events: swimming in the Tug River, hijinks at Halloween, slaughtering a hog, football season, etc. The setting is the tiny West Virginia coal-mining town of Crum — which actually exists — during the time of the Korean War. It is about friendship, sexual initiation and growing up. It is a traditional American young-man-coming-of-age novel.

The opening chapters blatantly embrace and embody just about every stereotype of Appalachian life that has ever reared its ugly head. "Life in Crum was one gay, mad whirl of abject ignorance,"(1) Maynard writes. "In the summer people busied themselves...dumping trash on the riverbanks and digging new toilet holes."(6) The tiny town is squeezed between river and hills, baked by heat, trapped by floods and has "the patience, good looks and energy of a sloth."(1) And, if we take the narrator's description of his friends and neighbors at face value, the people are fitting denizens of the place — mean-spirited and absorbed in practical jokes and sex.

All this is laid out in a very direct, very funny low style. The first part piles on one incident after another, like the stories people tell competitively, each person topping the last. And with each retelling, the tales get more and more outrageous. There are the "pig-fuckers" from across the river in Kentucky, who shoot at the West Virginia boys if their boats come into Kentucky water. There is a battle with an enormous dog that likes to drag swimming boys out of the river. Halloween in the town of

Crum is characterized not just by mischief, but by mayhem, and in the course of the novel, not one, but two outdoor toilets are dynamited. You'll never forget what Ruby Harmon does with the apple slice to keep the narrator interested, nor will you forget the academically challenged Benny Musser, who entertains himself by playing with his genitals at home, at school and on the road. Then there is the time the boys rob a meat truck, hide a couple hundred pounds of meat in a hole in the ground and eat themselves sick.

The list could go on and on. The stories have a tall-tale quality. The characters don't seem to have a lot of interior life. The incidents are extreme. Any individual story might be true — there are no ghosts or supernatural events here — but as a whole, they have an aura of legend. Even the narrator's parents are a mystery: "Nobody would ever tell me what happened to my parents, if anyone ever knew. They were just gone to their reward."(7) He has been handed from relative to relative, and is now living with his cousins — second or third, he isn't really sure which. The world of *Crum*, as we first see it, then, is slightly askew, slightly flattened and almost completely comedic.

But, just when you think you've grasped the tone of the novel, the narrator notices the beauty of the hills above Crum. "I loved autumn, the one season of the year that God seemed to have put there just for the beauty of it."(55) Also, even though the narrator has explicitly insisted that this is a world in which adults have little part, when the teachers come back to the high school he lets slip his affection and admiration for some of them and even for the subjects they teach — especially for Coach Mason. Coach Mason is small, tough, and caring. He takes the boys out of town for football games, and then on the way home gives them the experience of eating in a restaurant. The section called "Autumn" has an occasional touch of the elegiac in its tone, and the third part, "Winter," becomes almost serious. The hillbilly stereotypes begin to break apart as people become sharply individuated. They may both be citizens of Crum, but there is little in common between the wildly punitive preacher who chases the boys all over the town on Halloween and Coach Mason, who saves the narrator from serious injury. Somehow Ruby and Benny and even the

Constable's wife seem to have a kind of rounded presence. We get a glimpse not only of how they seem to the narrator, but also of how the world seems to them. We begin to realize that the narrator's protestations about Crum are not necessarily to be taken as fact. Indeed, we begin to feel the presence behind the narrator's voice of another voice, of the narrator as a man, looking back at the boy he once was. This ironic distance allows the narrator to be seen in perspective along with the people around him.

The complexity of the novel is clear in one of my favorite chapters, the second to center on Benny's penchant for making his privates public. A new teacher who delights in literature has large, much admired breasts. The narrator likes her a lot, but it is not clear if he likes the breasts or the literature. He probably doesn't know himself. Benny loves her, and the whole class joins together in happy expectation of screams and entertainment at the moment when Benny demonstrates his love. When he does, the teacher quietly begins to cry and leaves the room. In the aftermath, the narrator feels himself and his friends diminished. The jokes are less funny; the story becomes darker. Hilarity and tall tales are tinged with loss and sadness.

And in spite of the narrator's strong voice, the novel does not burrow down into his psyche, but it constantly opens up to include multiple world views. Benny may be dirty and more than a little disgusting, but his yearning for a soft place to put his face, and his innocent conviction of the value of his penis as a love offering, give him a wholeness and even an off-center kind of dignity. The narrator is thus a boy among others, a boy in a context, and the context is a group of boys and girls within the context of a town, and the town in its place in the hills. The novel is in the end a group portrait, a story that is perhaps not multi-voiced, but one in which all the characters are allowed a separate existence. The narrator's friends and nemeses and lovers are not so much objects in his world as subjects in their own right.

For me, the only false note in the entire book is its one dip into sentimentality. This happens in late winter, in the chapter about Yvonne (pronounced Yuh-vonne), the smartest of the girls, and the one who is in many ways most like the narrator.

She too wants out of town. The sentimentality does not come because she decides to finance her escape by trading sex for money. It does not come because she and the narrator try to connect and fail catastrophically. Rather, it occurs when the story forgets Yvonne's subjectivity. For a moment, ironic distance is lost and the mature narrator seems to agree with his teen-age self that he is the cause of some terrible disaster coming to poor Yvonne — that if only he had known how to love Yvonne, he could have saved her from a life of prostitution. In other words, the character of Yvonne is for the moment not about her own story, but is there to prove the narrator's moral sensitivity. The emotional clarity of the novel is dulled for that moment, but we are soon back to the narrator's litany of reasons to hate Crum, and the reader's growing realization that Crum is more than this litany.

I think this back-and-forth is why I like this novel so much. The narrator is convinced he hates Crum and has no use for his so-called friends and their trashy ways, and he gives us elaborate and hilarious evidence for his position. Yet, by the end of the novel, willy nilly, he is beginning to see differently, as we have known for a long time. A few days before he leaves town for good, he goes to the top of a hill famous among the boys as a place for defiant outdoor bowel movements in sight of, yet hidden from, the town and school. Here, he sees Crum as he has never seen it before. "The sun was directly overhead, flooding the valley with a sort of liquid illumination caused by the heat and the shimmer from the valley. The scene was more than I had ever known to look for.... The lanes of the town were perfectly straight and didn't have a bump in them. The river was crisp and sharp, a deep green color that looked pure and wholesome."(143)

Then, on the day he actually leaves, hitch-hiking by the side of the road with his cardboard suitcase, one of his friends comes up on a bicycle and offers money to help him on his way, to try and say good-bye. The narrator hangs tough and stays strong, refusing all offers of friendship. "Nip was doing just what I tried to get away from," he says, "making me feel there was something to Crum, after all."(157) He succeeds in getting away, but he feels — and the reader feels — bereft.

The novel, then, makes a remarkable journey from the opening descriptions of barren shacks to a rich human and natural landscape. In the end, Crum is abundantly supplied with oversized personalities and a folk history of legendary battles. The narrator protests over and over again that he hates Crum, but we see that he is leaving what he loves. There is no suggestion that he should *not* leave, only that he is severing genuine ties. This is one of the most quintessential Appalachian and indeed American experiences. So many of us are descendants of emigrants or have wrenched ourselves from our roots.

At the very end, the narrator of *Crum* recognizes partially and reluctantly what he is doing. The reader felt it long before and is terribly sorry to be saying farewell to faithful Nip, who commits a crime to save the narrator; to Mule, the friend who sometimes stands aside and lets the narrator get beaten up; to Ruby, who uses what little she has — her sexual hold over the hormonally overcharged boys — to carve herself a place in the world.

I have been told that at one time Lee Maynard was *persona non grata* in his old home town, that threats may have been made against his person. This may, of course, be one more tall tale or perhaps even a scurrilous rumor started by Mr. Maynard himself. It makes a good story, and a good story is clearly valued in the world of *Crum*. But in spite of any righteous indignation felt by the real people in the real town, I would contend that this is a novel about love of place. It explores and explodes its stereotypes. It is easy enough to think of Crum as ironic, as part tall tale and part coming-of-age novel, but I think it might also be called a love letter from a native son to his home place.

When all the goodbyes are said
I want to be the one who is leaving

And it's going to be good to be gone

SUMMER

Chapter 1

When I was growing up there, the population of Crum, West Virginia, was 219 human beings, two sub-humans, a few platoons of assorted dogs, at least one cat that I paid any attention to, a retarded mule and a very vivid image of Crash Corrigan. At first there were no whores, but later on I got to watch one in the Making.

"Crum — unincorporated" the road sign said, at the edge of town. It should have said "unnecessary." The place is located deep in the bowels of the Appalachians, on the bank of the Tug River, the urinary tract of the mountains. Across the flowing urine is Kentucky.

Life in Crum was one gay, mad whirl of abject ignorance, emotions spilling over emotions, sex spilling over love, and sometimes blood spilling over everything. The Korean War happened to be going on at the time, but it was something being fought in another world and, besides, who really gave a damn about all those gooks anyway. Our boys could handle them. Or so they said in the beer gardens. And what the hell were gooks? I had never seen one. Or a nigger. Or a Jew. Or a wop. I had heard those names from some of the men who had been outside of West Virginia, working in the steel mills of Pittsburgh and the factories of Detroit. But I didn't know what the names meant and I had never seen any of those people.

During the winters in Crum the days were long, boring and cold, and during the summers the days were long, boring and hot. In Crum, only the temperature changed.

The sad little town lay in a narrow valley, squeezed between the river and the hills, trapped before the floods, baked by the ancient heat of the mountains, awaiting each stagnant winter with all the patience, good looks and energy of a sloth. It was a collection of small houses, an assemblage of shacks, a reflecting pond of tin roofs.

The only paved highway into Crum came from downriver, from the general direction of Huntington. Actually, the road entered the valley by coming over the top of Bull Mountain, a dark and brooding hill that hung over the far ridge, closing off the valley. At the top of the hill the Mountaintop Beer Garden was penned between the ridge and the twisting road. Once past the beer garden, the road dropped into the valley like a dead snake. As soon as the road hit the valley floor it met the railroad tracks, a few miles downriver from the town. The two ran side by side from there on, seeming to be tied to each other, right through the middle of Crum and out the other end. The highway and the tracks stayed together until they were farther away from the town than any of us had ever ridden our bicycles.

If you drove down the highway from Bull Mountain and kept on going through town, the highway and the tracks divided the town into the hillside on the left, and the valley floor, across the tracks to the right. At the beginning of town a narrow dirt lane led off the highway and crossed the tracks and then followed the rails closely all the way through town, recrossing the tracks at the far end. The few people who lived along the hillside used the paved highway to come and go. The folks who lived on the valley floor used the dirt lane, and the even smaller dirt lanes that left it and ran off between the houses in the general direction of the river.

When the dirt lane first crossed the tracks on the way into Crum, it separated the tracks from the high school football field, with the school building sitting back across the field on the edge of the river bank. That school building was one of the first things you saw when you drove through Crum, and it was one of the places I always went when I was lonely. I could sit on the school steps and watch the cars go by — whenever there were any cars. And I could think about the people in the cars and wonder where they were going. I wanted to find out.

There were only a few houses along the hillside. Yvonne lived there, and so did Elvira. And Parson Piney had his house on the highest spot on the hill, where he could look down on everyone. I'm sure he thought God had ordered it that way. And the tiny house I lived in was there, tucked in between some trees and partially sheltered from view. But mainly the hillside was too steep. Most of the people lived on the flat valley floor, jammed between the triple routes of the highway, tracks and lane to the left and the river on the right. The houses began at the downriver end of the valley, just beside the high school, and continued upriver until they ran out of space, a distance that couldn't have been more than a mile.

Across the river was Kentucky, a mysterious land of pig fuckers.

About halfway through town, to the right of the tracks and just off the lane, was Luke's restaurant, the only restaurant in Crum. It wasn't much of a restaurant, just a square box of a building with bare light bulbs inside, a few wooden tables and some rough, handmade booths. But it was open at night and it had an old juke box. And a light on the front porch. There was no public lighting of any kind in Crum — "unincorporated" meant there was no public anything, no sewer system, no water system, and no real law except for the constable and now and then when a state police car rolled through town. But Luke's Restaurant had a light out front, and so it just naturally served as a focal point for the kids in Crum. Just a little beyond the restaurant, sitting back at the edge of a small grove of trees, was the town's only church, a lonesome, rickety little building. When you looked at it from the side, it looked as though a truck had run into it from behind, pushing the back of it up and in, the whole building leaning slightly, only we could never figure out in which direction.

After the church there was the tiny post office, and then Tyler Wilson's General Store. There, the dirt lane widened into a larger area so that cars could park in front of the store, a rambling, two-story building. There were heavy wooden benches on the front porch and, at sometime during the week, most of the older men would go down to the store and sit for a spell.

The railroad station, looking like a scale model, sat out on the edge of the wide parking area, snuggled right up against the tracks.

At the far edge of Tyler's parking area the dirt lane went back across the tracks and ended at the highway. And that was about all there was to Crum.

In the summer, when school was out, the town died. The teachers, the only people in Crum who could provide diversion and interest, left the town the day after classes ended. Almost all of them lived somewhere else and stayed in town solely because they had been assigned to teach there. For the most part, Crum was the only place the county school board would let them teach. Not because they were bad teachers, but because, for some reason or other, they were out of favor with the school board, usually because they refused to kick back part of their salary to the county political leaders. Of all the teachers in the high school only one or two actually lived in Crum the year round. The rest arrived a few days before school was to begin, rented a small house or a room or two, opened up their books, and taught. When classes ended, so did their stay in Crum. And you really couldn't blame them. The whole place was a mistake for them. The town was a zero. A blank. Nothing. All the cake walks, the school carnivals, pie socials and church meetings of the year couldn't make up for that. The teachers came and went like migrating birds in reverse, showing up in the autumn and leaving in the spring, but building no nests and sending forth no singing.

No one in his right mind would spend four years in college earning a teaching degree, just to come to Crum and teach. Many of those assigned to Crum refused and many of those who came just walked out after the first month or so. The school itself didn't help much, either. It was a twelve-year school, all twelve grades from elementary to high school in the same building. The halls were hard and hollow and the noise echoed through the rooms in great crashing peals. There was no gymnasium, no auditorium, not even a large meeting room. The library was a tiny, cramped room with two tables, eight chairs, a small desk, a collection of Zane Grey books and for some reason a subscription to the NEA Journal.

And there were no indoor restrooms. Crum High School had what might have been the world's largest outhouses, two of them, thirty yards out behind the school. It was enough to drive you nuts, it was enough to drive me nuts, and it sure as hell drove a lot of teachers nuts. They didn't stay long. They just didn't stay long, and I used to watch them get in their cars and drive away and wonder where they were going and how many other places they had been and why they had ever come to Crum in the first place. God, how I used to wish that I were one of them, that I could climb in a car and drive away.

Crum really was lonely when school was out. The teachers were gone for the summer. Nine out of ten of the kids rode the bus to school and just weren't seen again until the following September. All the buses were taken to Wayne, the county seat, and parked in the school board bus lots until the next school year, row after row of long yellow vehicles sitting in the sun. Almost every autumn, when they were getting the buses ready to go back into use, they would find where some kids had gotten into one or two and done a little drinking and a little fucking. Beer bottles would be lying around in the aisle and on the seats, and a few used rubbers would be hanging from the steering wheel and the rearview mirror.

So action in Crum in the summertime was limited to the few kids who actually lived there. There was Ruby Harmon, Nip Marcum, Wade Holbrook, Cyrus Hatfield, Yvonne Staley, Elvira Prince, Mule Pruitt, Ethan Piney and Benny Musser. And sometimes that sonofabitch Ott Parsons. And a few others, now and then. Some more girls, of course, but the only girl I think I ever cared about was Ruby Harmon. I would get tired of the same people day after day, and I would spend long days by myself, exploring the ridges, playing in the river, foraging in the hills, finding small streams and trying to follow them to their source, locating the hardwoods and the nut trees where I knew the squirrels would be when hunting season came around, looking for deer and wild turkey sign and every now and then discovering a pack of wild dogs. Sometimes it was a good time in the wilderness around Crum and sometimes it was not, but it was always lonely.

I'm not really complaining about being alone in Crum. Most of the time I *wanted* to be alone. I thought most of the kids in Crum were my friends, but there were a few I wasn't really sure about. Ethan Piney was one of those. I don't know how it was that Ethan and I got to want to kick each other's ass so much, but that's the way it always was. If there ever was a line drawn, you can bet that Ethan and I would be on different sides of it.

And there were some kids who weren't my friends, and they weren't my enemies. They weren't anything to me, and I wasn't anything to them. They didn't give a damn if I was there or not, or if they ever saw me again. When school was in session, they were just there, taking up seats, faces in the classroom. I hardly ever saw them when school was not in session. I knew that they lived in Crum and didn't come to school on the bus, but I didn't know where they went or what they did. I didn't know who their families were. Some of those kids just seemed to disappear.

In the summer people busied themselves in Crum by dumping trash on the river banks and digging new toilet holes. Early on they planted a few sugar cane patches down on the flats just above the river, hoping that the last high water had come and gone. Along about May, the town's only gas station would pour a winter's collection of oil drippings on the driveway and the oil would seep into the ground, collecting dust and spreading its smell. Little kids played in abandoned cars, using them as forts, houses, schools, cars, whorehouses and a thousand other things, then took stones and broke every scrap of glass out of them. Trains steamrolled through town, throwing smoke and cinders and bringing the town to its knees by the sheer size and sound of their passing. In the summer in Crum the river would go down and the springs would dry up and the people would talk about their wells. With no water system, no sewer system, no systems of any kind, the heat of an Appalachian summer would bring the outhouses to their full ripeness and spread the pungent aroma up and down the narrow Tug River Valley.

Some of the houses had electricity and a few had bottled gas but for the most part they were just a collection of boxes strung up and down the railroad tracks. The hills came down to the tracks, and across the tracks the flat, narrow valley floor spread gently toward the river, then dropped off sharply to the river bottom. And across the river, Kentucky.

My house — on the hill above the valley — wasn't "my" house exactly. I mean, it was their house, the house of my second cousins, Mattie and Oscar, I think, or maybe they were third cousins. I was born in Turkey Creek, a holler up on the north edge of the county. (Those narrow spaces between the ridges and the hills are "hollers" — not hollows, or canyons, or anything else.) Nobody would ever tell me what happened to my parents, if anyone ever knew. They were just gone to their reward. After a while I stopped asking about it. I was handed from relative to relative, from holler to holler, until I was old enough to be sent to Crum where I could go to school. Until I was raised, they said.

My relatives in Crum were an ordinary bunch, for Crum. Mattie was the woman of the house, a large, dark, hard working woman. During the day, Mattie sometimes worked in Luke's Restaurant, helping Luke cook whatever there was to be cooked that day, and trying to keep Luke's dirty hands out of the stuff that he was going to feed to the customers.

Mattie's husband, Oscar, was a miner, and the nearest mine was some distance away from Crum. I don't really know how far. I know that Oscar left the house early and got back late. He would scrub himself at the mine right after quitting time, then come home and go out back and scrub again, trying to rid himself of the grime that collected around his eyes and in the creases of his hands. He scrubbed out back even in the winter.

I thought that Mattie and Oscar were a lot older than my parents would have been. They had a couple of children, both girls, but they were grown and gone from home, both of them having gone off to Williamson a long time ago to get jobs and to live in a town that was bigger than Crum. I used to see the girls sometimes around holidays, but then they got married and Mattie and Oscar would go to Williamson for the holidays and I would stay in Crum, alone.

In fact, there were a lot of days when I never saw anybody around the house, only the heat from the wood stove telling me that anybody at all had been there. But that was okay with me.

After the girls had left home, Oscar and Mattie had moved into a smaller house, tiny, with only one bedroom. It was the house they were living in when I showed up. The house was perched on the upriver end of Crum. A narrow porch ran along the front and around one side, reaching back to the shed that was tacked onto the back of the place, the shed where I slept and kept all my valuables, the shed that was mine. The shed was the only thing they could afford to let me have. But it wasn't their fault; they had already raised their kids, and one day they had been sent another one, one they had never seen before. That's the way things go. All things considered, I was luckier than most kids.

The folks in the house didn't bother me much, and I didn't bother them. They fed me if I was hungry and they made sure that I got to school often enough to keep from being kicked out of the place, but it was not their job to raise me. I was raised already. I was old enough to go to high school.

When I think about it, I guess I never paid much attention to them, and that seemed okay at the time, for all of us. Most of the kids in Crum never paid much attention to the grown-ups, unless they had to because of trouble. Mostly, we just kept to ourselves, doing our things and letting the grown-ups do theirs. We all seemed happy enough with that arrangement.

Summer seemed like the day after Christmas, when you have had something just a little nicer than the rest of the year but now it's over and there is some sort of empty feeling that won't quite go away. And you want badly for it to go away and you work at it but nothing seems to help. Just suddenly it's gone and you don't know why and you are caught up in summer in Crum and it's lonely.

There were a few regular weekly events that seemed to help regulate a town which needed no regulation. There was the weekly arrival of the meat truck from Huntington. It made two stops, then went on its way to Kermit. It seems odd but I never ever saw the meat truck on its way back to Huntington. I used to watch for its arrival in Crum because it was a sign of outside life and of other people doing things. But after it left for Kermit I never saw it return. I guess it went home by another route, but I knew the road maps by heart and I could never figure it out. We stole a load of meat off the truck once, and the driver never knew how he lost it. We stole so much that it rotted before we could eat it all and we would sit, gorging ourselves, trying to keep ahead of the spreading green rot, only to finally throw most of it in the river.

Another weekly event was the moving picture. There was a building in town that had been a general store, then had been converted into the Masonic Hall. The ground floor was one large room and every week Aaron Mason, who was a teacher and coach at the high school — about the only teacher who lived year-round in Crum — would show a moving picture. Because his name was Mason, we always thought that he owned the Masonic Hall.

The moving pictures were rented and came on the mail train, and the only pictures Coach Mason could afford to rent were the old Westerns. Those were the ones all the kids liked anyway, so there we were, with television taking over big cities like New York City — only we didn't know that — and we were growing up with Hoot Gibson, Tom Mix, the Riders of the Purple Sage, Ken Maynard, Al Fuzzy St. John, Gene Autry, Roy Rogers, Sunset Carson, the black hats and the white hats and gunfighters who could sing. Autry and Rogers were relative newcomers and not nearly as popular as the other cowboys. During the movies the kids would yell and scream and throw trash at the screen when the villain was doing okay. And everybody believed in everything, particularly the heroes. There was a hero named Crash Corrigan, a big cowboy who could lick everybody in sight and who was one-third of a trio called The Three Mesquiteers. And Crash was our local hero. Little kids called themselves Crash and local make-believe gunfights always had a Crash who stood up alone against everybody else.

The only other regularly scheduled event in Crum during the summer was Mean Rafe Hensley's weekly drunk at the Mountaintop Beer Garden. Mean Rafe would get it going on Saturday afternoon and by late Saturday night he would be out in the middle of the highway, shooting a pistol at the moon and challenging all comers. When Mean Rafe went outside, everybody else stayed inside, and when he reeled his way back inside the beer garden, everybody else cleared out the back door.

We would stand outside and look in at the greasy tables and dirty floor, the rows of coolers behind the bar. Selling whiskey across the bar was illegal in West Virginia then and if you wanted the hard stuff you had to sneak it in yourself, or buy moonshine from the bartender. The 'shine was served in water glasses, or sometimes in old fruit jars. The bartenders wouldn't sell good whiskey because the 'shine made a hell of a lot more money for them. And besides, it was pretty damn good moonshine. We could see Rafe, a glass of 'shine in his hand, standing dead center in the middle of the floor, laughing and shouting and scaring hell out of everybody. Sometimes he'd go out to the middle of the highway and shoot at the moon. We all hated him. We all wished he would drop dead or get run over by a truck. At least once his pickup truck got hit by a rifle bullet as he drove to the beer garden, but the bullet didn't touch Rafe and he would point out the hole to you as a sign — I'm not sure of what. But all we ever did was stand outside and look in. It just wasn't safe to mess around with Mean Rafe Hensley on a Saturday night.

There were no other regularly scheduled events.

In the summer, the sun beat down on nothing much. It scorched the vegetable gardens that everyone had just outside their houses. It burned the drowsiness into the people and out of the flies. The early morning mists and the sun and the evening light as soft as cotton were a part of most every day.

Sometimes it would rain. There is nothing softer than a quiet rain in the mountains, warm, musical and clean, coming from air that has been scrubbed and polished. When I used to feel that I was really closed in, when I felt that I had about come to the end of my string, when I felt that if I had to look at five more minutes of Crum I would just lie down in front of the next train . . . usually when I felt that way, for some reason or other it would rain. The rain would close in my world, bringing it down to a small gray dome that moved with me as I walked through the hills and hollers. Nobody else stirred much in the rain. They huddled against the damp, waiting for the drops to cease their drilling against the tin roofs. They didn't smell the peculiar smell that you can smell just before a rain. They didn't hear the sounds that can happen between the drops. They never heard a bird sing in the rain. But I did. I loved to prowl the hills and the town in the rain.

In the summer in Crum the world died. I would wait through the long months until autumn brought whatever spark of life there was to bring. Maybe it was the teachers. I like to think so.

Of course, there were a few bright spots during my life in Crum, such as fucking in the cane fields down by the river on warm, sunny afternoons, and the day we robbed the meat truck, and the day that Constable Clyde Prince's outhouse exploded, and beating the living hell out of Ethan Piney. And Ruby Harmon.

Chapter 2

Ruby Harmon was really something. She knew things other girls didn't. For instance, she had a bra on every morning when she left the house — I mean, her mom would have never let her out of there without it. But then she would sneak into a closet at school or go out to the outhouse and take it off. And she would be sure that all the other girls knew it. Then she would lean over my desk and brush her nipples against me, walk down the hallway just close enough to make people understand that she was my girl, play me off other guys just to make them jealous, use me in every way possible and then not let me in her pants. I loved her.

I loved her, but she was the most conniving woman that I have ever been close to. Ruby had one goal in life — to be the most popular, the best liked, or at least the most woman in whatever she was doing at whatever time in whatever place. When she got here, Ruby moved into our gang the way a bitch dog in heat moves into a pack of hounds.

We weren't a real gang. We were just a dumb bunch of kids forced together because we all lived in Crum; we had no one else to hang out with. But none of that mattered to Ruby: she wanted in, and she got in. At school, shortly after she moved into town, Ruby quickly sorted things out. It was amazing. She just seemed to know without working at it. She knew that the kids who called the shots around there, for the most part, were the ones who lived in Crum, who did not ride the bus to school. She knew that Mule and I and Nip and Ott and Cyrus were the guys to contend with, and that we could get away with almost anything we wanted. We decided who played the games and who didn't, who was class queen, what clothes were worn by those who had a choice and who did and who did not go home at the end of the school day with all his teeth intact.

Ruby knew that Nip Marcum was the one who seemed to be always there, but always on the edge, in the center but not really, the one who was never challenged because there didn't seem to be much to be gained by it. Nip was smaller, deeper, and probably smarter than the rest of us. He was never the king of the group, but when I think back about it, he probably was the one guy who held the whole bunch together.

Ruby knew that Ott Parsons was probably the plain meanest of the bunch, whenever he did see fit to hang around with us. She knew that he was bigger and older than the rest of us, that he was not too smart and had been held back a couple of years in school, that he was always, *always*, looking for a fight, and that his older brother, Ralph, was certainly at least a little bit crazy.

Ott Parsons. Jesus, sometimes I don't even like to think about Ott Parsons. There are just some guys who are better left alone, and Ott was one of those. He loved to fight, loved to pick on smaller kids, loved to lie to his older brother — and usually those lies were something made up just to get the rest of us in trouble with Ralph — and we didn't need any help to be in trouble with Ralph. I think Ott was a thief, a real thief, not like the kind of thief we all were when we robbed the meat truck. Anytime anything was missing, Ott always seemed to be mixed up in it. Fortunately, Ott really didn't hang around much. Maybe we were just too tame for him.

The only guy that Ott never really gave any shit to was Cyrus Hatfield. Cyrus was the strongest guy in the group, straight shooting and upright, and the one guy who, if you did force him to fight, would kick your ass until you couldn't walk — and then spend an hour telling you he didn't really mean it.

Ruby hated little Benny Musser, really hated him. She just refused to acknowledge that he even existed. That always puzzled me. I mean, just because Benny was a dirty creep who liked to walk around with his pants unbuttoned and his dick hanging out didn't mean that he couldn't be part of the group.

And in Crum, there were stranger kids still. Like Ethan Piney. I hated Ethan Piney twice as much as I thought possible. In every group there's one guy that you just know you'll never be able to like. Ethan was my choice for that job and I was his. Ethan was the son of the local preacher. The preacher was a fat asshole who used to show up in my nightmares — and sometimes in real life — trying to rip off my head.

Wade was big, fat, lazy, and mysterious. He lived in Crum, but not really. He really lived out behind the Mountaintop Beer Garden where the road went across the top of Bull Mountain. We saw a lot of Wade because the beer garden drew us to it with a force that we could not resist. Wade said little, did little, but when he did manage to get something going, it usually caused one hell of a racket. If I ever have something that I want to blow up, I want Wade to help me do it.

And then there was Mule Pruitt. I guess I never really understood Mule, and I don't think Ruby did either. Maybe nobody did. Mule was supposed to be, at least on the surface, my best friend. We were always together, always in the wrong place at the right time, always trying to figure things out so that we came out on top. I used to think that we looked out after each other, but I'm not really sure. Maybe we were friends just because we were the most alike. Maybe we were friends just because we were always one good fight away from being enemies. Maybe we just had no choice. All I know is that when we were together we would try anything to relieve the monotony of living in Crum; we had that much in common, at least. But I seldom heard Mule talk about leaving. Me, I talked about it at every opportunity, but Mule never said much. I guess it just wasn't important to him.

I tried for years to figure out how our gang worked and I guess it was sort of like a bad stew. The boys were the tasteless chunks of things floating around in the pot, mostly unidentifiable, but sort of gristly if you bit into them, with the girls as the spices and the heat.

Ruby took over as queen of the girls the day she moved in, but the other girls never really accepted it. I don't think Ruby really had a girl friend. She had boy friends, friends who were boys — and that included all of us at one time or another — and the whole world wanting to get into her pants. But she had no girl friends. She wouldn't allow that.

Elvira Prince had a better all-around body than Ruby and she was one of the first girls I ever knew who liked to fuck and did not care — honestly did not care — who knew it. Elvira was choosy about who, though. She liked to get hot and she liked to roll anywhere she felt like it; but only some guys could get in her pants. Benny was one of those, but not in the usual way.

Yvonne Staley was the only truly beautiful girl in Crum. Yvonne had dignity, a presence, a way of seeming destined for better things than Crum. She was the quietest of the girls and certainly the smartest. Nobody ever said that Elly was smart, they just said that she liked to fuck. And Ruby was smart, but smart like a fox is smart, crafty, always looking one step ahead for the next trap. Yvonne was different.

Actually, there was a fourth girl. No, not a girl. A woman. She was a woman who seemed always to be in my mind. But she was married and never, ever, hung out with us. Genna was sort of Elvira's mother or, more, her stepmother. She was the constable's wife and she was the sexiest woman in Crum, or maybe anywhere, and she could make any of us feel like insects.

Ruby picked me out pretty quickly. It wasn't that I was the strongest guy in school, because everybody knew that Cyrus Hatfield had it over everybody when it came to muscles. And I wasn't the fastest. That was probably Mule, when the sonofabitch would really run. And Benny was the guy who would start the most trouble, just by doing what he liked to do most — playing with his dick. Ott Parsons was the one who was just plain meanest. So I don't know why Ruby picked me out except that maybe I could do a little of everything, that I could be a little like all those guys, and I seemed to be able to figure my way into and out of things without getting my ass in a permanent sling. So I was her target.

There were three things that most every kid in Crum High School had in common — poverty, ignorance and fucking. We were dirt poor and didn't know anything about anything outside the Tug River Valley, but we all knew about fucking. Everybody fucked somebody.

Half the girls in school who rode the bus home fucked some guy in the back seat on the way. They used to take turns in the back seat because the bus driver had a hard time keeping track of things going on back there. There were days when

I would sneak on the bus and ride it downriver, just to get in on the action. I'd have to hitchhike back to Crum and, since there was really very little traffic on some of those roads, sometimes I would have to walk part of the way. Once, I didn't get home until it was time for school to open the next day.

Ruby Harmon used sex better than anyone else, even though I never knew anybody who Ruby fucked, at least not in Crum. She moved to Crum from down in Tennessee and that alone was sort of exciting. She had red hair that she would comb out long and let hang down around her shoulders and the breeze would catch it as she walked from the school toward home on windy spring afternoons. You could tell it was her from half a mile away, her hair was so real and so red and so soft. Sometimes she let me run my fingers through it, especially when other guys were around. One day a bunch of us were loafing out back of the school, lying in the shade and listening to the insects buzz in the heat of the summer. We were doing nothing in particular, since there was nothing in particular to do. I reached over and ran my fingers through Ruby's hair. She looked up at me and smiled — and then she looked at the other guys. Ethan Piney was there and he had the hots for Ruby, almost as bad as I did, and it really pissed him off to see Ruby and me play around.

Ethan was fairly tall and pretty strong, but as long as I knew him he had a tiny little belly that rolled over his belt and I always wanted to punch that little roll. I promised myself that someday I would. His old man, the Reverend Herman Piney, had more than a little roll. He had a stomach that held enough food to allow the good reverend to fight the devil for weeks at a time. The Pineys lived in a house that sat high on the side of the hill overlooking Crum, and Ethan thought he was hot shit because of that house. And hot shit because his father was a preacher and made Crum writhe in hellfire every Sunday morning. The Reverend Piney was one of the world's truly fat men, and when you looked closely at Ethan you could tell that he might be on his way to becoming as fat as his father.

Ethan walked over and put out his hand to touch Ruby's hair, but she grabbed his wrist. His face got red and he was ready to do something, so I stepped up to find out what he might have in mind. I was eager to show off in front of Ruby.

"Shit," he said. "It don't mean nothin' anyway. It probably ain't even real red." He snorted and walked off slowly. To walk off fast would have been a retreat. To not walk off at all would have gotten him a smash in the face, or at least a punch in that little roll over his belt. So he walked off slowly.

Ruby looked at me and then at the other guys. "Do you think it's real? The color, I mean! Do you think this is my real color!?" She shouted the words, first at me, then at the group.

"Sure, Ruby," I said, "I mean, I know that's your real hair . . ."

No one else said anything.

Ruby was mad, madder than hell. Instantly. She turned to face me. "Look," she said, "you better believe that this is the real color of my hair, and I'll prove it to you! You can tell those other bastards all about it!" And she whipped up her skirt. She was wearing the whitest panties I had ever seen, with lace around the legs. She grabbed the panties at the crotch and pulled them to the side. The hair was only about a shade darker red than the hair on her head, and it looked sort of packed down, like her panties were too tight. She held her panties to the side for a second or so, then let them go. They sort of snapped back into place and she let her skirt fall. There were two or three other guys standing around and none of us moved. I was pretty sure they couldn't have seen a thing, and they were just as sure that I had been close enough to kiss it.

"I hope you got a good look at that," she said, "and you can tell the rest of those bastards that it will be a hell of a long time before any of them *ever* see it! Bastards!" She loved that word. "Bastards!"

God, I loved her. She had shown me her pussy on the school grounds in front of two or three other guys, and I was big stuff around there for a while. And it sort of started something. That was the first time Ruby had done anything like that and I think she got to like the idea. For the next month or so she would take my hand — when she knew someone else was watching — and pull it over under her skirt. She would rub it on her leg, then like a shot she would ram it into her crotch and then out again. I never really got a good feel, but the very idea that she had done such a thing made me want to fall down and roll around on the ground. And whimper a little.

One hot day in late August, Ruby asked me to come to her house for a birthday party. She lived in a house by the railroad tracks near the middle of town, next to the church, and she liked to sit out on the front porch and watch the people walk down the dirt lane, on their way to the post office. A bunch of her relatives from Tennessee were visiting and they had brought with them a big, blond, mouthy sonofabitch from Ruby's old home town. He was an old boyfriend of Ruby's, and it was his birthday party. Right away I didn't like him. Ruby had invited me to the house just so she could show the big sonofabitch that she hadn't wasted any time after she got to Crum. Well, that was one time I wasn't going to play the game. I was pretty damn mad about the whole thing and I was just about to get the hell out of there when Ruby caught on to my intentions. Without saying a word she took my arm and pulled me into the kitchen, making sure everyone saw. She pushed me back against the washstand and kissed me long and hard. The kiss didn't take very well and Ruby knew it. She was in danger of blowing her whole deal and it panicked her a little. I had always played the game before but I was in a real bad mood this time. Ruby kissed me again, this time running her tongue around inside my head. Her tongue tasted like quick taffy in the sunlight and that usually did the trick. But this time I was so damn mad that she had to come up with something else, and pretty fast.

There was a basket of apples sitting on the kitchen table. Ruby backed off and stood there for a while, looking at me. I thought she was going to cry. She glanced around the kitchen, saw the apples and moved over to the table. She picked one up and held it to her face, looking at me over the top of it. She took a bite, then held it out so that I could bite right on top of where she had bitten. I bit.

I stood there munching on the bite of apple, looking at Ruby, frankly wondering what she would try next. I was getting interested again. Ruby opened a small drawer in the side of the table and took out a paring knife. She split the apple in half, then cut a slice off one of the halves. I was still chewing my bite. She pulled up her skirt and pulled her panties over to one side. My eyes were glued to that red thatch. She leaned back against the edge of the table, letting me have a good look. She must have taken a bath just before the party because her hair stood out puffy and soft. Ruby put the apple slice into the hair, carefully snuggling it into her slot, as though it had been made just for that. Then she let go of her panties and her skirt and everything was back to normal.

I was hooked. I just couldn't believe it. The slice was still in there. The rest of the evening I behaved like a trained dog. I did everything and anything that she wanted me to do. I co-operated, I waited on her, performed. All I could do was think about that slice of apple. And the big, blond sonofabitch couldn't figure out what was going on.

At about midnight the party broke up and Ruby went to the front porch with me. She was very pleased with the way I had come through for her and she kissed me several times. She shoved me toward the steps, slipped something warm in my hand, and was gone back inside the house. I looked in my hand as soon as I got out to where the moonlight was bright enough to see, but I knew what it was. The aroma from that apple slice nearly drove me mad. I took it back to my house and kept it in a crack in the wall of the shed where I slept. I kept it there for weeks until it was dried and crisp. And even then I imagined that I could smell Ruby there. Of course, I thought about eating it. I thought about it all the time, but, for some reason, I just couldn't. When the slice was so dry that it lost all its smell, I took it to school with me one day and put it in with a bunch of other dried fruit pieces that they were serving in the cafeteria. At the end of the lunch hour all the pieces were gone.

Chapter 3

The dog was the biggest sonofabitchin' dog I had ever seen.

Living in Crum, where the dogs were either mongrels or some sort of coon hound, you just never saw a really big dog that had long — or even medium-long — hair. The German shepherd that belonged to Ott Parson's brother sure as hell wasn't any coon hound.

As I said, it was the biggest sonofabitchin' dog I had ever seen. Ott's brother, Ralph, had picked up the dog in Germany, a few years after the Second World War. Ralph was a lot older than most of us and he had already been in and out of the Army. The dog, too. He had been in the German Army, according to Ralph.

Ralph was a lot like Ott. He was big, mean, not too smart, and could lick anybody in town. I don't know if he could lick Mean Rafe Hensley — especially if Rafe was drunk — or if he could lick Ott, but he thought he could. And that's the way the dog was, too. The only difference between Ralph and the dog was I guess the dog was probably a little smarter.

He was a rescue dog, trained by the Germans to pull objects out of the water. Any objects. Even people. One of Ralph's favorite games was to sneak up on a bunch of us when we were down at the river swimming and turn the goddamn dog loose. He'd see all us objects floating around in the water, and he usually thought that he had found the meat store. He would ram his huge body into the water and make for the nearest kid, grab him by the arm, leg, or whatever he could get hold of and drag him bodily out on shore, usually half-drowning him in the process. Whenever we saw Ralph and the dog coming we would swim over to the Kentucky side of the river and get out on the bank. We'd be stuck there, Ralph and the dog on the other side, until Ralph got bored and took the dog away.

We hated Ralph and we hated the dog, but there wasn't much we could seem to do about it. Fighting with Ralph was a sure way to lose some teeth, and doing anything about the dog was practically impossible since he was always with Ralph. We had even thought of poison, but we probably would have had to poison Ralph first to get at the dog.

It was a real pain in the ass, being run out of the river like that. Especially for Nip, the slowest swimmer. The goddamn dog was always getting to Nip first. Sometimes, his arm would bleed from where the dog had grabbed it and we'd have to take Nip back to my shed and rinse his cuts off in fresh water from the well and tie some rags around them. Nip never got rabies, so I guess the dog was healthy. But crazy. Once when the dog grabbed Nip by the arm and started pulling him toward shore, Nip fought back. He began to pound the dog on the head with his free arm, screaming and thrashing in the water. The dog shifted his hold and grabbed Nip up at the shoulder and it looked like he was going to bite Nip's arm off. The other guys yelled and waved their arms, but the dog wasn't paying any attention. I was closer to the shore than the dog so I scrambled to the edge of the river and ripped a heavy branch from a dead tree tangled in the brush at the edge of the water. Nip's eyes were rolling back in his head and I knew he was in pain, but I didn't want to get too close to the dog. I steadied myself in the slow current and took aim. The branch circled over my head and I brought it down with everything I had. It cracked the dog dead center between his shoulder blades. He opened his mouth in a shriek that made the hair stand up on the back of my neck. And he let go of Nip. The dog sank into the water and disappeared.

Jesus, I felt like a hero. None of us had ever had the guts to hit the dog before, and now I had done it. Nip was crying and holding his upper arm, but the dog was gone. Everything was going to be okay. And then I realized that Ralph Parsons was screaming at me and wading into the river and that the dog had surfaced about three feet from me and was swimming straight at my balls.

Everybody started yelling at once. We splashed wildly, throwing water and foam and raising all the hell we could. Everyone yelled at Ralph to call off the dog. It was time to get the hell out of there. I leaped over backwards and twisted, hitting the surface of the water flat on my face. I stroked downriver as hard as I could. I figured I could out-swim the dog, but I wondered if Ralph would run along the bank and cut me off when I got to shore. I swam hard for as long as I could. When I eased up and took a look behind me, I was around a small bend in the river and there was no one in sight. I eased out of the river, sneaked into a cane field, and got out of there. I would be safe back at my shed. Ralph was tough on the river bank, but he would never go to anyone's house.

I hated that fucking dog even more after that.

Actually, I guess none of us were supposed to be swimming in that damn river. They would tell us at school that the water was polluted, and that we would die if we swallowed any of it. I never saw an adult swim in the river, but then none of us ever really saw adults do much of anything that we would have considered fun. Going swimming, going in the river, was something to do, and best of all it was something that we knew the girls would not do. Sometimes they would come down to the river and watch, but they never swam. Except one girl. And one time. And of course that girl was Ruby.

She and I had been sitting on the upper river bank, throwing rocks into the cane field below and watching a hawk soar over the ridge high up and beyond the Kentucky bank. I took her down the bank and through the cane field to the edge of the water. We sat for a while, just staring out across the river. It was times like that when Ruby was almost human. I mean, she was always human, but she was also always acting, putting on some kind of show, leading me around by the nose, or just plain getting mad and ripping hell out of whatever happened to be handy. But this time she was nice, and we talked, and it was one of the best times with Ruby I can ever remember.

But I couldn't leave the situation alone. I started trying to get her to go into the water and to go swimming with me. I took off my shirt and my shoes and waded out into the brown stream. The river must have been rising a little because it was picking up more silt. When I had waded in up to my belt I looked down and realized that there was so much silt in the water that you couldn't see into it. I took off my pants and threw them up on the river bank.

There I stood, naked in the river, everything just out of sight below the brown water. Ruby was fascinated. She stood up and the light shone through her thin cotton dress, outlining her legs and giving them shape and form even beyond what they already had. I kept up a steady stream of quiet talk, coaxing, almost begging, trying to get her to come into the water.

She moved forward slowly. Her feet slid in the sand and she seemed to drift toward me and down until she was in the water up to her ankles. I think she knew that the sun was shining through her dress because she kept her legs farther apart than she needed to. I couldn't help letting my eyes drop and every time I looked up she was staring directly into my face. She knew exactly what I was looking at. She knew exactly what I was thinking.

She eased into the water up to her knees. And then up to her crotch. She cupped her hands and dipped them into the river, raising them dripping to her chest and cupping each water-filled hand over a breast. When she took them away her dress was stuck to her breasts and her nipples stood out hard against the thin, wet cloth. She bent her knees quickly and gracefully and then straightened again, soaking her dress all the way up to her waist. When she stood up her dress was stuck to her body, a thin covering of transparent cloth that hid nothing, nothing at all. This time, I thought.

I took a single step toward her, toward more shallow water, my body rising slightly. Her eyes drifted from my face down my chest to the water, now just barely covering my thighs. I was just reaching out to take her arm when her head came up and she looked, puzzled, past my right shoulder. Then her expression snapped instantly from puzzlement to revulsion. She slapped her hand over her mouth and spun away, splashing violently toward the bank.

I whirled around. Floating gently in front of me, moving lazily on the soft current in the gentle afternoon light was a horse, a bloated, long-dead, stench-producing, gray horse. Its inflated stomach bulged upward and kept it partially on its side. Something had eaten away part of its skin and the shoulder bone showed through. Its neck was bent slightly upward, exposing one dead eye to the sunlight. The dead eye was looking at me.

From behind me Ruby gagged, a constant, deep retching that seemed to come all the way up from her toes. But I couldn't take my eyes off the horse. I had never seen anything like it. Even for the Tug River this was something special, the ultimate floating insult. It was absolutely fascinating. I watched until the horse quietly drifted around the bend in the distance and the gray mound of the horse's stomach was no longer visible above the soft brown of the silted river.

When I turned around Ruby was gone. And she never, ever, as far as I know, went near the river again.

Every time the dog would pull Nip out of the water, Nip would lie there on the bank and stare at the dog and at Ralph, Nip's eyes looking pained and hurt, seeming to ask, "why the hell can't I swim in this river without your fucking dog ruining things?" We felt sorry for Nip, but it was his problem. We were faster swimmers.

Mule Pruitt wanted to shoot the dog. I had a single-shot .22 rifle that would do the job, and I was a good enough shot to get it done without Ralph seeing who had done the shooting. But if I did it myself, the rest of the guys would always have something that they could tell Ralph if I ever got out of line, and so I wouldn't do it. I agreed to furnish the rifle if somebody else would do the shooting, but nobody agreed.

And so we were stuck. We sat around dreaming up complicated plans to get rid of a dog that would pull you out of the water, grab your arm, tear your flesh and rip your hide, not let go until you had been dragged onto the bank, and generally scare the living hell out of you. And none of the plans were any good, none of them would work, none of them would allow us to get away with it, and all of them would provide Ralph with a reason to beat hell out of us, one at a time, and then one at a time again. But Nip had been thinking, and his plan was pure, simple and brilliant. All it really required was a little bit of fast water.

The Tug River was quiet in the summer, almost stagnant really, and low enough to walk across in most places. That was why we swam mostly around a big rock on the Kentucky side — it had a deeper pool of water near it, deep enough to swim in even when the river was very low. It was huge and black with a steep downstream face and a gentle climb up the back side. Once on top the rock made a great diving platform, but you had to be accurate enough to hit the small pool just below. In the spring and autumn the rains would come and swell the river, the water rising up the banks and picking up the garbage and trash that people threw there knowing it would get carried off. Now and then though, even in the summer, a rain upriver would produce a quick rise in the water, and for a few days the water would be too swift to swim in and we would have to settle for sitting on the bank with slingshots and rifles, taking random potshots at floating bottles, cans, turds, partially-inflated rubbers and other interesting items that floated within range. Ralph and the dog would usually be there.

Ten days after Nip announced his plan, the river began to rise. It hadn't rained in Crum but it must have been raining somewhere upriver because the water had come up a couple of feet — just enough to put some snap in the current but not enough to prevent swimming. Nip made sure that Ralph knew we were going swimming. Not that he wouldn't have been there anyway — Ralph and the dog didn't take any chances.

Cyrus Hatfield had been selected to do the swimming. He was the best swimmer among us, and besides that he was stronger than hell and if anything went wrong where the dog was concerned, Cyrus was a decent bet to be able to muscle his way out of it.

I was still a little worried about Ott, Ralph's brother. Naturally, we had not said anything to Ott about what we were going to do to Ralph's dog, and I thought that when Ott found out he would try to do something about it. Like kill one of us, just for the fun of it. But it was too late to figure out what to do about him, so we just went ahead with the whole project.

Sure enough, Ralph sauntered up with the damn dog at his side, eager for the chance to haul somebody's ass out of the river. He found us huddled there on the river bank. Nip let out a low moan and announced that he might as well go home, nobody was going to go swimming with that fucking dog around. Ralph grinned. He figured he had screwed us again. Wade Holbrook agreed with Nip and the two of them walked off into a cane field upriver. The plan was for them to double back downstream and run like hell to the spot Nip had picked out.

Cyrus stood up and walked slowly to the edge of the river, wearing only his shirt and his ragged overalls. No shoes. He was ready. The dog tensed, its ears upright and pointing in Cy's direction. The entire scene was a familiar one to him. He would wait.

We watched Cyrus approach the water, the fresh current sweeping away from in front of him. There were many trees along the river bank, and Cyrus was standing in a gap in them, on the downstream side of the gap. Suddenly he leaped into the river. It was a long leap, designed to carry him as far out and as far downstream as possible. He hit the water feet first and immediately began stroking. The current pulled him quickly downstream. The dog had been coiled, waiting, and the second Cyrus hit the water the dog was up and in the air. The trees prevented the dog from running along the bank to catch up with Cyrus so it had to leap through the same gap in the dense growth that Cyrus had used. The dog followed in hot pursuit as Cyrus got swept behind the screen of trees.

Ralph rolled over on the sand, laughing his damned ass off, visualizing the scene that would take place as soon as the dog caught up to Cyrus, how the dog would sink those big teeth in. Only the dog didn't catch up to Cy, at least not while Cy was in the water. We had counted on Cy being able to outswim the dog, and he did. But he made sure the dog saw him leave the river, and the dog made for the spot. When the dog got there, there were Nip and Wade standing knee-deep in the water. Wade had a rope in his thick hand, the other end tied to a heavy log that floated next to the bank. The log had one of Nip's shirts and a pair of his pants tied around it, and Nip was placing a long pole against a notch he'd cut in the log. When the dog got close enough, Wade let go of the rope and the two of them shoved the log into the current right in front of the dog's nose. The shove didn't get the log out as far as they thought it would but it did the job. The current caught it and began to pull it downstream, channeling it farther and farther into the middle where the water flowed faster.

It had taken six of us to trim that log and get it to the edge of the river. It must have weighed hundreds of pounds and we thought it would take that goddamned dog a long time to get it back to shore. And it must have. The last Nip and Wade saw of the log and the dog, the dog had caught up to it about a hundred yards downstream and was in the process of sinking his teeth into it. Then they disappeared around a bend in the river.

We never saw the dog again. He must have drowned or pulled the log over to the Kentucky side of the river and been unable to find his way home. And the funny thing about it was that Ralph never said anything about it. He really had no proof that we had done anything at all, and while that ordinarily wasn't enough to stop Ralph from beating hell out of us, he never really knew who to beat. He thought that Wade and Nip had gone home, and Cyrus has sauntered calmly back to the group after his swim in the river, inquiring casually where the dog had gone. The dog just disappeared.

We celebrated for a week. The only time we had a pang of doubt about whether or not Ralph would find out the truth was when Ethan Piney, the preacher's son, heard the dog had disappeared. He wasn't on the river bank — he was never a part of the group when we had anything special to do — and so all he knew about it was what he could pick up around town. But he began to figure it out. Somehow, he knew, we had made that goddamn dog disappear.

Ethan let it be known that he wold be willing to forget about the dog, and about saying anything to Ralph, for a price. When Cyrus heard about that, he went a little nuts. We had to sit him down and talk to him for a couple of hours just to keep him from killing Ethan, or at least breaking a couple of his bones. It took Cyrus a couple of days just to cool down, and when he got good and calm, good and cool, he took an ax, climbed the hill to Ethan's house one Sunday morning when Ethan and his family were at church and calmly chopped about three feet off Ethan's front porch.

We never heard anything more from Ethan about the dog.

A couple of years went by. Ralph had picked up another dog by that time, but there would never be a dog like the shepherd. In fact, Ralph became known as a man who collected dogs, who would steal dogs. He kept them all at his house, under his house, outside his house, inside his house. Some people said that he had thirty or forty of them at one time. They slept on his bed. He fed them, all of them, in his kitchen. He broke the windows out of a spare bedroom on the corner of the house and put some old crates underneath on the outside. That way, the dogs could climb up on the crates and come and go through the bedroom windows any time they wanted.

On a chilling, damp, mid-winter day when a layer of low clouds closed off the top of the river valley, when the thin plumes of smoke rose from the chimneys, when Crum was quiet, Ralph gathered all the dogs inside his house and locked the doors. He sat in the middle of the living room floor — there was no furniture in the living room; more room for dogs that way — and gathered the dogs around him. Probably thirty dogs in one room. Then he lit the fuse on a stick of dynamite and stuck the thing in his mouth.

Chapter 4

Acouple of weeks after we killed off Ralph's dog, a bunch of us were sitting out on the front porch of Luke's restaurant. It was a late afternoon in mid-summer, it was hot, and we were drinking cold soda pop and trying to figure ways to make money. Inside, Luke was fixing meals for a few customers, raking hot dogs out of the kettle of boiling water with a long fork. He held the fork in one hand and picked his nose with the other. Luke would then wipe his fingers on his apron and use the apron to hold the bun in which he placed the steaming hot dog.

Luke served other stuff too, mostly plates of pork chops, pinto beans and cornbread. Now and then there were fried potatoes and pork side meat. And you could get cold buttermilk. There wasn't a menu. You just ate whatever Luke happened to have cooked that day — not the hot dogs if you could help it.

Luke was okay. He was a short, thin, little man, with stringy hair that kept falling across his eyes. His face was divided by a sharp nose that stuck straight out and he had crooked teeth, and some of them were missing. He walked with his shoulders slouched, which made him seem smaller than he really was, and when he waited on a customer at the counter, he would stand on a pop case turned upside down so he could look people in the eye.

But Luke was okay. He never ran us off the porch, and if we really wanted to, we could always find something to do for Luke that would earn a nickel, or maybe even a quarter. Making money was a big thing to us. We all knew that life would be a hell of a lot easier if only we had some money and it would be ours, all ours. It was a symbol, a physical thing that was interchangeable for anything, as long as you had enough of it. And no kid in Crum had ever had enough money. All I knew was a kid who had a dollar — a single dollar — was very nearly rich. And he could make that dollar last all week.

Money was important to other kids, but it was even more important for me. For me, money was one thing and one thing only, but a thing I thought I would never have — a ticket out of Crum. I used to read library books and make lists of all the places I would go when I had made enough money. I might even go to Chicago or to New York. I knew more or less where they were, and I thought that they were big enough that I was bound to hit them if I just pointed myself in the general direction. I could understand some of the smaller cities that I read about, but I could never understand New York. How could any place be that big? How could any place have that many people, more people than in the entire state of West Virginia? I wondered if there were any deer or rabbits there, and if any of the kids hunted. I wondered if they ever camped out overnight or if they swam in the river. None of the books said anything about that. I really couldn't understand New York.

On the top of my list of places to see was the Grand Canyon. I didn't know too much about it, but I knew that I wanted to see it. And I knew that it was in some state out west. Maybe Ohio.

Yvonne Staley sat with us for a while. Her shining black hair and huge brown eyes went with her dark complexion. A long time ago I had heard Luke tell one of his customers that Yvonne's family was part I-talian. I told the other guys, but none of us had ever seen an I-talian and we didn't know whether being part I-talian was good or bad. And none of us had the balls to ask Yvonne about it either.

Yvonne always behaved too right for Crum, if you know what I mean. When she crossed her legs she never let them slip apart just to give the guys a quick look. She never played up to the guys and she never played down to them either. They were just there, and she was just part of it. It was like she was just passing through.

She also had a lot of brains. She was in our class and we knew that school work never bothered her. She always had her homework done early and had plenty of time to go to the school's tiny library and read. Maybe she was just too smart for us.

Wade Holbrook used to say that he was in love with Yvonne, but that lasted only until a black winter night out behind the school after a school cake walk. He had caught her on the way to the outhouse and grabbed her from behind playful-like, just to see what she would do. When she didn't make any particular effort to get away, Wade turned her around and pressed his huge stomach against her and stuck a hand under each of her cheeks so that he could pull her against him, pull her against the bulge in his pants.

Wade told us about it later. By that time, he thought the whole thing was pretty funny. He said that she went sort of limp and then said, "Wait, let me fix my coat."

He loosened his hold and she stepped back, unbuttoning her coat and spreading it open. Wade couldn't believe his eyes — or his luck. He ripped open his own coat, the cold air rushing in under his shirt. When his coat was nice and open, Yvonne stepped back and carefully kicked him in the balls. Wade went down like a beached whale, lay there on the ground for about half and hour and damn near froze to death.

Yvonne — we pronounced it Yuh-vonne and so did she — sat quietly at Luke's restaurant. She seemed interested in the money talk. One idea to make money was scrap iron. Wade said we should gather more scrap iron for when the dealer came back. We had been sitting down beside the railroad track one afternoon about a year before when a guy in a huge truck pulled up on the highway across the tracks. He got out and came over to us, which was amazing in itself. He wanted to know if we knew where there was any scrap iron he could get his hands on, and we said that there might be but that he would have a hard time gathering it up. He made a deal with us — if we would gather up the iron, he would pick it up and pay us for it on his next trip through Crum. We agreed. We could see his truck was full of pieces of metal including a couple of old cars and we figured he was a real scrap iron dealer.

The scrap iron we knew about were the pieces along the railroad track which dropped off trains. Old spikes, nuts, bolts, strap metal and things like that. We went to work gathering them up. We gathered up anything that was loose and that looked remotely like iron and stored the stuff in the old barn behind Benny's house. We must have walked a hundred miles of track picking that stuff up and carting it to Benny's. Then we turned the town upside down to make sure we hadn't missed anything there. We worked our butts off for about two weeks, and the sonofabitch never came back. We never saw that truck again.

Mule and I beat Wade over the head with our caps and Benny kicked him for mentioning scrap iron. Wade rolled down the steps and lay there at the bottom, on his back on the gravel, his stomach rolling up at the sky. The day was so warm and lazy that we could get away with it. We talked about selling other things, only nobody could think of anything to sell. We could sell bottles — we could return them to Luke's restaurant for the deposit — except the little kids in Crum had that job cornered and you couldn't find a bottle to return anywhere. We couldn't go to work, not in the usual jobs. We were too young for the mines and there were no jobs in Crum that several grown men weren't waiting in line for.

So we sat there, just drinking pop and talking. After the pop was finished, Ruby had to go home and then Wade and Benny drifted off after a while, seeing that there would be no money-making ideas today, leaving the rest of us with our warm, empty pop bottles in our hands. Once Ruby left, Yvonne got more talkative. She kept talking about money, and how much bus tickets cost, and how far you could go if you had a hundred dollars. She was wearing a pair of her brother's jeans. They were too small for her, pulling up into her crotch. Mule was staring and Yvonne seemed to know it, only for a change it didn't seem to bother her.

We had been talking about getting money and leaving Crum and what we would do if we could do that, and I don't remember seeing Yvonne so interested in anything. I had never known that she wanted to leave until that day, and it sort of surprised me to hear her talk about it. She had some pretty strong ideas.

Mule was a born troublemaker and finally he just couldn't help himself. I guess the sun got to him. He sat up and looked straight at Yvonne.

"Could I feel your cunt?" He said it quietly, almost as though he were waiting for Yvonne to belt him, or something. Nip almost fell off the steps. I was sure that Yvonne was about to issue one of her lethal kicks to the groin.

"How much do you want to feel of it?" She spoke quietly, with a halt in her voice. Mule blinked. He had really asked the question because it had been quiet for long enough and he thought that by asking Yvonne to feel her cunt he would really be starting something.

"I want to feel it a lot. I really want to feel it good."

Yvonne sat there, thinking about it. Finally, her words came very slowly and carefully. She said quietly, "How much would you pay to feel it?"

She looked at Mule, then at Nip, then at me. It was quiet again in front of the restaurant and the hushed tones of the questions and answers seemed to add to the stillness.

"I ain't got but thirty cents," Mule mumbled.

"Okay," she said, "you can feel it for thirty cents."

Mule stood up and dug out the thirty cents, held it out to Yvonne. She let the coins fall into her hand, then sat looking at them for a moment. Mule sat down beside her and reached for her crotch.

"Not here. Around behind the restaurant." She got up and walked quickly away. Mule was right on her heels, and then Nip got up to follow. I was going to do the same.

At the corner, Yvonne turned and looked at Nip. "Not unless you've got money," she said softly. Nip stopped dead in his tracks. Yvonne looked at him for a second, then turned and went around the corner of the building, Mule close behind.

A couple of minutes later Yvonne came out from behind the restaurant. She walked past Nip and me, glanced unsmiling in our direction and walked away down the dirt lane in front of the restaurant.

"It's hard as a rock! It's hard as a fuckin' hot rock! She's got the hardest pussy I ever had my hand on!" Mule said.

I grabbed him and pulled him down to the steps. "Did she say anything about fuckin'? Did she? What did she say? Can you buy it?" I kept shaking Mule by the arm.

Mule just looked at me. "Five dollars," he said. "Five dollars."

I looked away and after Yvonne as she grew smaller in the distance down the dirt lane.

She really was good-looking, and it was hard as a rock.

Five dollars.

Five dollars.

Yvonne had found her ticket out of Crum.

Chapter 5

Mule came back to the shed with me and we sat around talking. He rolled some old corn silk and we smoked it, feeling good as the darkness rolled over the mountains, covered the river and then eased up the other side of the valley, until the window in my shed went black.

All he could talk about was how hard Yvonne's cunt was. For two days we talked about it, and about whether or not Yvonne really would fuck her way out of Crum.

How to make some money became an obsession with us. It was all we could talk about. And we were talking about it a couple of days later when we happened to wander into Tyler Wilson's general store. Sitting by the pot-bellied stove was a basket of coal.

If the river was the bowels of the town, the general store was the heart. It was a real general store — it sold everything. And if you didn't want to buy anything, it was still a good place to go and sit on the front porch, just to watch the other folks come and go and maybe to get a bit of gossip for your trouble.

And Tyler Wilson was just the man to run it. I used to stand by the counter and look up at him. Tyler always wore his hat, even inside the store, and he was so tall that it almost touched the ceiling. I had seen a picture of Abraham Lincoln in a book at school, and I always thought that Tyler Wilson must have been taller than Lincoln. And he had the same face, deep seams running in all directions and never changing except when he laughed.

And he was smart. He could add things up in his head and tell you the exact amount, and if you got a pencil and did it for yourself you found out that he was always right. We guessed he had a lot of money but nobody knew for sure. He lived up over the store in some rooms that, as far as I know, nobody ever saw. At least no one that I knew was ever in them. Most of the people in town liked Tyler. I wasn't one of them. I was a little afraid of him.

It was summer and the stove was cold, but there was this basket sitting there full to the brim with coal. I picked up a piece. There was hardly a chip or crack anywhere, the edges worn smooth and even, the pieces of coal polished like with a fine hand and an emery cloth. There wasn't a speck of coal dust in the basket.

"What do you think of that?" Tyler asked. "Bet you never did see coal like that before, not in West Virginia. No, sir, not here in West Virginia. Our coal is all soft and dusty. This coal is fine." He drew the last word out to make it last, to make sure we knew this coal was different.

"Where did you get it, Mr. Wilson? Did somebody polish it up special for you or something?" Mule asked.

Tyler just laughed. "No, sir, boys, that coal came out of the Tug River, right off the bottom. Reckon that river's been shinin' that coal for a whole lot of years, to get it all smooth like that and all. Bought it yesterday from a feller come through here with a pickup truck of it. Paid him half a dollar for that basket."

We looked at the basket in wonder, half afraid of what we were hearing. "What will you do? Will you burn it come cold weather?"

Tyler was still smiling. "Well, now, I reckon I might just do that, if it gets a might cold in here." He pointed around his store. "Mighty nice coal to burn, too. No dust, no bother in the room. I like that. But, if I burned it, wouldn't have no more shiny coal for folks to look at. Don't rightly know what I'll do with her, but right now she's pretty good for lookin' at."

We looked at Tyler, then at each other, then without saying a word we turned and left the store. Tyler grinned, his tall frame moving slightly, satisfied that he had another showpiece for the town to come and look at. Every month or so he would have something in his store like that. It was his way of bringing in the customers, which was sort of funny since Tyler had just about the only store in town. The other little store at the bus stop wasn't much more than the size of Tyler's front porch, but Tyler always felt the competition was out to get him.

Mule and I went straight to Nip's house. He lived at the top of the river bank, on the far south end of town, but not too far from Tyler's store. And he had a boat. It was a flat-bottomed john boat built years before by Nip's father. It was old and full of holes but we thought we could fix it up and use it. The river was pretty shallow in most places now and the thought of getting all those half dollars for all those baskets of shiny coal we could pick up was just too much to resist.

Nip, Mule and I got the boat up on the bank and went straight to work using an old can of roofing tar. We turned the boat over and put Nip underneath. He would point out the holes and Mule would dab a glob of tar on them. I was keeping the tar hot on the fire. Once a glob went through the hole and landed on Nip's stomach. Nip screamed, kicked at the side of the boat and tore the toenail off his big toe. By the time the toe had stopped bleeding a blister had formed on his belly, but he was calmed down and he went back under the boat. He was a tough little kid.

The boat was ready in no time at all and we shoved her into the water. Mule scrounged some rope and I found a rock and we made an anchor. We cut poles from small trees growing along the river bank, and we shoved off.

The current was sluggish and the poling was easy. We went downstream until the river widened out a little and the water spread over a nice, soft sand flat. We could see black specks on the bottom every now and then and we thought they were pieces of coal. As we neared the Kentucky side the black spots got thicker so we kept going until we were no more than five yards from the Kentucky shore. We threw out the anchor and Mule and I slipped overboard. On the first dive, I found a piece. Mule found two. Treading water, we threw the pieces into the boat.

Nip was excited with our luck. "Man, we can go all over Crum! I bet everybody'll want a basket of this here coal to set in their parlor. We're gonna be rich!" Mule and I dived again. Most of the black spots were just unidentifiable crud and it was almost fifteen minutes before either of us found another piece of coal.

The going was slow and the work was hard but in about two hours we had a sizeable pile in the middle of the boat. I was getting pretty tired. I dived for one more piece, came up and saw Nip standing up in the middle of the boat. He didn't say anything, just pointed toward the nearby shore. Two Kentucky boys were sitting on the bank, staring quietly in our direction, a large stock of rocks between them, piled like cannonballs. Those rocks didn't grow there.

One of them, a tall redhead, stood up. "We figure that to be our coal you got there, hillbilly, seein's how you got it closer to our bank than to yourn." He spoke it out easy, each word pointed right at me.

Before I could say anything, I heard another voice come banging across the water, hard and flat. "If you want this fuckin' coal, come in here and try to take it, you Kentucky cornholer!" It was Mule, partially hidden by the end of the boat. "You go to hell, you dumb pig fuckers!" Mule added for good measure. I was standing where my feet could barely touch the bottom of the river, in that limbo where the water is just about to lift you off your feet.

The tall kid reached down and picked up a rock, letting his arm hang at his side and swing just a little. "I'll tell you one more time to give over that coal . . ."

Before he could finish Mule shouted "FUCK YOU!" and began to haul up the anchor. I figured I had better swim for it and just as I turned over backwards in the water a rock smacked into the river a few inches from my head. I dived so hard I hit the bottom and damn near surfaced again before I could straighten out my thinking. I swam underwater in the general direction of the boat, listening to other rocks sploosh into the river. I surfaced, grabbed some air and dived again, my legs sticking up in the air for a second as I went down. A rock glanced off my shin and I yelled, water rushing into my mouth and strangling me. I lost my air, had to surface, tried to grab my shin and rub it, saw another rock coming and got back underwater just in time. By that time, Mule had gotten the anchor loose. I think he untied the rope, but may have just pulled the rock out. The boat started to drift off downstream and in a few minutes we were out of rock range and Mule and I climbed back into the boat. Another couple of minutes and we had poled our way farther across the river and were out of danger. But Nip was missing. We were looking around the river for him when we heard a voice from our side of the river. It was Nip, yelling from the bank. We poled over and picked him up, then poled back out into the river again, coming back to a spot just out of rock range. We held the boat there with the poles. The two Kentucky pig fuckers were still there, yelling about their coal. Every now and then one of them would pick up a rock and throw it as far and as hard as he could, testing the range. We were about six feet beyond their best throw.

So we stayed there for awhile, yelling insults back and forth, showing them the pieces of shiny coal we had. All of a sudden, we couldn't see them. It was a strange sort of business, and after they were gone we sat there feeling the letdown that sometimes comes after an exciting string of events. My leg ached, a large bruise beginning to show. For probably twenty minutes we didn't say a word, using the poles to hold the boat against the easy current, feeling the sun and listening to the water suck against the bottom of the boat.

It was a calm day, the sun ballooning its way toward the tops of the trees, the air silent and quiet, our backs drying in the heat. Mule, Nip and I contemplated the shiny pieces of coal in the bottom of the boat and the size of our fortune. In the midst of trying to figure out all the money we would make a shot crashed across the river and shotgun pellets sprayed water into the boat.

For an instant no one moved. We just looked at the bank, trying to see what the noise was and where it came from. We knew it was a shotgun but we just couldn't believe that someone was shooting at us because of a few pieces of coal. The next shot hit the water, the boat, my right arm and Mule's chest and there was no use pretending any longer. We dropped the poles and the three of us hit the water at the same time. I swam underwater downstream for as long as I could, trying to angle in toward the West Virginia side, thinking that probably they would be waiting for us to come up in line with the shore. When I came up for air, I chanced a look at the boat. It was closer to me than I thought, then I remembered that we had no anchor and the boat was floating free. We would lose it. It was headed for the Ohio River and Cincinnati with our fortune aboard, and another shotgun blast reminded me that to try and stop it would only bring more lead flying my way. I went under again and headed for shore, pulling myself out of the water and in among the slimy tree roots. I felt that I was safe, and I crawled up the bank and into the weeds, lying quietly. The shotgun couldn't reach me there, but I wanted to take no chances.

I was wet and I was cold. I began to crawl farther away from the bank. I could hear some thrashing around in the weeds to my right and I crawled toward the sound, found Mule, holding his chest, rolling around in the weeds and moaning into the mud under his face as he rolled over and over. There was lots of blood and I figured that he was going to die and I wondered if I would ever get the chance to get even with those pig fuckers who were probably still sitting on that other bank laughing and pissing into the water.

Nip crawled up and we turned Mule over. He had six small holes in his chest with little black pellets sticking in them. When I saw the tops of the pellets, I knew Mule wasn't going to die, after all. A trickle of blood came from each tiny hole. Nip calmly took one of the pellets between his fingers and squeezed underneath it until it popped out. Jesus, I just don't think I could have done that. When he was finished with Mule, Nip took my arm and squeezed out the pellets. All the tiny holes bled more, but at least the pellets weren't in there.

We made our way back to town, not saying much, wondering how trouble like that happens, how it gets started. It was odd for us to wonder that because we knew that we had started our share, only now we were on the wrong end of things. As we passed Luke's restaurant, Yvonne came out carrying a carton of soda pop. We stopped and said hi to her. She nodded, said nothing, and went on toward home. She looked strangely hard to me. Perhaps I had just never noticed before, but she did look hard now. I still didn't know anybody who had actually paid their five dollars but I guess now she was a whore and I guess she knew it.

Nothing much happened after that. The little holes in our bodies scabbed over and festered, then healed. I was rinsing my wounds with cold water one evening when Oscar came home from the mine and saw me out there. He looked at the little scabs and I think he knew what had caused them, but he didn't say anything. The next morning I found a small jar of salve sitting on the porch outside my shed.

I stayed away from the river for almost two weeks. Then I forgot about the whole thing. One hot, late afternoon I went down on the river bank with my old .22 rifle and threw cans into the water, trying to shoot holes in them before they filled with water and sank. I looked up and there on the Kentucky bank was a guy watching me. I couldn't tell if he was one of the two or not. I looked at him for a while, then raised the rifle and pointed it in his direction. He started, gathering his feet under him, tensing. But he didn't run. I guess he figured I wouldn't shoot. I took careful aim and drove a slug into the mud near where he was standing. He tumbled over backward, more from surprise than anything else, the jumped to his feet and disappeared into the brush.

I was going crazy. What the hell was I doing? I left the river and climbed the bank, my mind reeling. I knew then I had to get the hell out of Crum, I just had to. Maybe this would be the last summer. Maybe next summer would come and I wouldn't be here. Maybe I would be the one to be leaving. It would be good to be gone.

Chapter 6

It wasn't long from our coal-collecting experiment to the day that Mule and I decided to rob the meat truck. There was no real reason for it — we weren't hungry, but we'd been handed our asses by those Kentucky pig fuckers and we needed something to make us feel good again. Plus, we needed something to do — the summer days stretched emptily ahead.

The meat truck came from Huntington once a week and made two stops in Crum on its way to Kermit. It dropped over the ridge at the top of Bull Mountain, at the Mountaintop Beer Garden, gear-ground its way down into the valley and made its first delivery at the little store by the bus stop. That store never bought more than a roll or two of lunchmeat and it only took the driver a few minutes. He would get out of the truck, unlock the small doors on the back, take out the meat and disappear inside the store. Soon he would come back out, climb into the truck, drive across the railroad tracks and onto the narrow dirt road that went past Luke's restaurant and on to Tyler Wilson's General Store. He usually stopped at Luke's place for a quick drink of Nehi Orange. He didn't lock the truck doors again until he came out of Tyler's store.

I said we weren't hungry but I guess in a way meat was sort of valuable to us. Meat, all the meat we could eat, had never been had by any of us. Usually we ate meat two or three times a week — pork side meat, bacon, jowl, and whatever other pieces of the hog could be had for near nothing. We had an egg or two for breakfast with some bacon, and you could eat a hot lunch supplied by the government in the school's small cafeteria or you could bring your own lunch in a paper sack. At supper, though, it would have been nice to have meat all the time, but we seldom did. It just cost too much. There were days on end when supper was a collection of potatoes, beans and whatever other vegetables that were cheap at the time. Even Mule, whose dad was one of the best pig killers around, mostly ate only the leftover parts of the hog. And we almost never got to eat any cow.

At Mattie and Oscar's house every month or so we did get some beefsteak. We would get the toughest steak that money could buy and then take a hammer — a real hammer — and pound the living hell out of it until it looked, felt and smelled like the aftermath of a slaughter. Mattie would then cook the bloody remains for hours over a low fire in the wood-burning stove. She'd make brown gravy and bring the whole thing to the table in a large pot, the steak bubbling in a pond of hot gravy and sending out a smell that made you hungry enough to eat your belt. There would be potatoes and green beans, sliced tomatoes and cucumbers, biscuits and homemade jelly and pitchers of cold milk from one of the neighbor's cows. And if you were lucky, there would be apple or blackberry cobbler for desert with more milk and pots of coffee. When you ate it you knew you had eaten something real. You lingered over it until you just couldn't hold any more, and then you just sat and remembered it for a while. That monthly ration of steak was like Christmas. You looked forward to it and when you knew it was *the* day you would hang around the house just so you wouldn't miss any of the smell. The smell from the stove would come straight through into my shed and I would lie there for hours, reading my books and scribbling on my scraps of paper and just smelling that incredible smell.

Mule had never eaten steak until I brought him to the house once for the big meal. I thought he was going to cry. All the Pruitts *ever* ate in the way of meat was pork — after all, Mule's dad was a great pig killer. For months after that all Mule could talk about was how he was going to buy steak when he had the money, buy steak until he was smothered in the red, slimy, raw, bleeding stuff. I guess that was one of the reasons we robbed the meat truck.

We had a clubhouse down on the riverbank. We had dug a huge hole into the clay and sand in the middle of a thicket of brush and scrub trees, had covered the front and part of the top with boards we had picked up along the river, had covered the boards with cardboard and old pieces of canvas, and then had thrown dirt and sand over everything. It made a good clubhouse, but it sure as hell was dark in there. We made candles and we would sit around in the clubhouse talking and laughing in the wavering light and listening to the river gurgle. It always seemed comfortable, no matter how damp or chilly it got. Probably that's because the place was ours and only we knew where it was. We never even told the girls, although actually they knew anyway. In fact, maybe everyone knew, though we didn't know it.

When we decided to rob the meat truck, Mule and I dug another small room at the back of the clubhouse into the cool earth deeper into the river bank. We planned to hide the meat in there, saving it until we had rested up again and could eat some more. We planned to go up into the hills with part of it and have a big feed up on the hill that overlooked the town, which we called Shit Hill. We also planned to take some of the scraps, swim across the river and dump them on one of the trails over there. That way if the law came looking for the meat the trail would lead over to the Kentucky side and put the blame on some of those Kentucky pig fuckers.

Mule and I figured it would take more than the two of us to do it the way it ought to be done, so we got Nip and Wade to help. We thought about Benny, but he'd probably get too excited and screw everything up. Cyrus Hatfield would have been better but Cy was simply too honest. Cy was strong and would fight anybody at the drop of a hat, but he just wouldn't steal.

So we got Wade and Nip and explained the whole thing to them. The plan was simple. The truck would stop at the bus stop and the driver would unlock the doors on the back. After he made his delivery there, he would get back inside, drive the truck across the railroad tracks and head for Luke's restaurant. The dirt road on that side of the tracks was never in very good condition. No one maintained it and the mud holes and ruts sometimes got so bad that ordinary cars just couldn't make it. The truck would have to go *very* slowly. It was a half-mile to Luke's from where the truck crossed the tracks. As soon as it was across the tracks, one of us would leap out of the bush alongside the road, run behind the truck and climb onto the small platform on the rear. Then, he would unhook the back doors, slip inside, and begin throwing meat out of the back of the truck. The others would be placed along the road ready to pick up the meat. If the driver got wise and stopped the truck, it was every man for himself. We had to get the whole thing done in the first quarter-mile after the truck had crossed the tracks because that was the only place where the banks were high enough and the brush thick enough to hide the operation. Besides, after that, there were houses along the road and it would just be too risky.

Wade volunteered to get onto the truck and throw out the meat. We argued about that, because we thought that Wade wouldn't be able to move fast enough to catch it. In fact, we were surprised that Wade wanted in on the robbery at all, since he hardly ever got his ass out of the chair on front of Crum's one television set, up at the beer garden where he lived. But the thought of all that meat was enough to make even Wade move his butt.

Mule would be the first to pick up the meat, then Nip, then me. Wade would jump off the truck and pick up the last pieces himself. We knew the meat would be in chunks and we were going to pick them up in gunny sacks, each of us carrying whatever was flung out into his area. We would meet at the clubhouse, store the meat, and go up to Shit Hill behind my shed for our first big feed.

On the day the truck was supposed to arrive, the four of us were down by the school, rolling around in the grass on the football field, soaking ourselves in the summer sun. We were there a good two hours before the truck was due. We tried to be calm, talking in low tones, not moving enough to show our nervousness, generally acting as though this was old stuff and we robbed meat trucks every day. But we were all excited and we knew it. Nip was so wound up that he was giggling, rolling around on the ground and making spitting noises between giggles. The closer it got to the time for the truck to arrive, the worse Nip got. Finally, Wade and Mule sat on him, hitting him with their caps and punching around on him until he got mad and settled down.

After a while we just lay there on the grass, watching birds ease their way through the air, listening to the afternoon insects make their particular noises, and getting hungry at the thought of all the meat we would soon get to eat.

Nip saw it first, downriver where the road cuts into the edge of the hills. The truck was on its way to the little store at the bus stop.

We headed for the dirt road, each on a separate route. Wade walked straight through the bush toward the bus stop. Mule dropped about a hundred yards back and hid in a thicket at the edge of a narrow, bumpy spot where the truck was sure to be going very slowly. Then Nip, and then me. We settled down to wait, each of us deep within his own fantasy, each of us dreaming of sides of beef, huge rump roasts and sirloin. I eased out toward the edge of the road. I could peer through the brush and see all the way to the crossing. It really wasn't very far away. I wondered if we would have time to get any meat off the truck. I readied my gunny sack.

The truck thumped its way across the railroad crossing. I could hear the gears chunking and grinding all the way at my hiding place. I watched the spot where Wade was hiding. As the truck passed, Wade leaped out from beside the road and disappeared behind it. The big meat robbery was underway.

The truck crawled toward Mule and I wondered if Wade had been able to get the small doors open. It got to Mule but still no meat was coming out. Instead, I saw Mule jump from beside the road and disappear behind the truck, just as Wade had done. Something had gone wrong. Mule was supposed to stay where he was, waiting for Wade to fling out the meat. If he got too far out into the road, the driver would be able to see him in the rearview mirror. But Mule jumped right into the middle of the road.

Then I saw why. Back down the road, a few yards from where he had been hiding, Wade was flat on his gut in the middle of the road. He had caught up to the truck okay, but he had lost his footing trying to swing himself up on it and creamed himself on the little platform on the back. Mule had thought fast and taken over Wade's job. He was determined to get the meat, and Wade could damn well lie there and bleed for all he cared.

As the truck moved forward I couldn't see Mule and I knew he had gotten inside. The truck neared Nip and as soon as the cab passed the spot where Nip was hiding, he popped out into view at the edge of the road, gunny sack in hand, waiting for the meat. It wasn't long in coming.

A flicker of motion at the back of the truck sent a giant slab of bacon sailing through the air. It struck Nip squarely in the chest and Nip and the bacon flew backwards and disappeared into the brush. What a hell of a mess. One guy lying bleeding in the middle of the road, another knocked ass over false teeth into the bush with a slab of bacon wrapped around his ribs, one on the truck sailing meat out into the countryside, and there I was, alone, thinking about how the hell I would ever pick all of it up.

The truck was gathering a little speed, now. The road was getting better and the driver was in a hurry for his Nehi. I could see some packages and stuff flying out of the back of it and I tried to remember where most of them landed. As the truck passed me I eased to the edge of the road and waited.

Nothing happened. The doors on the back of the truck were still open and I thought I could see someone inside. If Mule was still in there I didn't know what the hell he was doing, but he didn't have much more time to do it. The truck was nearing the first house.

I forgot about picking up meat and was lost in watching the truck. Suddenly, two figures appeared on the little platform, locked together, clinched tightly and lurching with the movement of the truck. One of them was Mule. The other was a full side of beef. The beef must have outweighed him easily, and he had the stuff in a death grip, wrestling it to the edge of the platform. They teetered there for a moment, the truck bouncing down the road nearing the houses, Mule and the slippery meat dancing madly back and forth to the bounces as though they were enjoying the ride in the warm afternoon sun.

But not for long. The next big bounce launched Mule and the meat out into the air and they crashed onto the road. The meat hit first and then Mule hit the top of the meat, bounced off and rolled across the road. He was covered with blood and beef fat and as he rolled he picked up dirt and gravel and dust from the road. You couldn't recognize him.

Mule was up instantly, grabbing the side of beef and dragging it toward the nearest thicket. I knew he wouldn't be able to carry it. We would have to drag the damn thing all the way to the river.

I came out of hiding and began working my way back down the road, looking for meat. I found some almost at once and shoved it into my sack. It was wrapped in shiny brown butcher paper. I couldn't tell what it was but I wasn't going to waste time finding out. I looked back over my shoulder toward the truck. It was still heading for Luke's restaurant and Mule and his meat were nowhere in sight. It looked as though we had gotten away with it. I went back to my meat gathering. The next thing I found was a bucket with its lid half popped off. The bucket was full of liver. I shoved the thing farther into the brush, covered it with some leaves and hoped the dogs would find it. I wasn't going to carry liver all the way back to the river bank.

A few minutes later I bumped into Nip. He was crawling along the ground, gunny sack in hand, gathering meat with one hand while he kept the other pressed against his chest. I figured he had some cracked bones in there, but he was keeping on with the robbery. I had to give him credit. I peeked out into the road. There was no more meat out there — Mule had flung it all into the brush — and I couldn't see Wade, either. Nip and I got all the meat we could find and took off, half carrying and half dragging the heavy sacks.

It took Nip and me more than an hour to go the half mile to the clubhouse. We crawled in through the tunnel and lit some candles, stashed our sacks in the cold meat storage room, covered up the entrance to it with some boards and settled down to wait for Mule. And for Wade, if he was still alive.

Wade was the first to arrive. He was covered with cuts, and cinders and gravel were sticking to his skin from when he hit and rolled. He had a couple of small packages of meat with him, picked up at the edge of the road before he figured he had better get out of there. I knew where the first meat had come out of the truck and figured Wade must have crawled more than fifty yards through the brush to get it.

We waited for Mule. The sun went down and the air around the river began to cool. The clubhouse was warm from the candles and our sweating bodies but we stayed inside afraid to leave our haul. When a couple of more hours went by we went looking for Mule. We didn't find him on the route we thought he would have taken to get the meat from the road to the clubhouse. We fanned out and looked some more, but wherever Mule was he didn't want to be found and so we didn't find him. A little later we gave up and went home, agreeing to meet back at the clubhouse for breakfast the next morning.

I was back on the river bank before the mist had time to clear off the water. I came down off the hill where my house was, headed straight for the river, then turned upstream after I was sure that no one had seen me. I made my way through the brush, drifted trash, cane fields and low-hanging trees. As I got closer to the clubhouse I slowed down and crept forward cautiously, thinking that maybe someone found the meat and was staking us out. But all I found was Nip and Wade, glancing nervously up and down the river bank.

"Man, you guys sure must have got up early," I said.

"Yeah, we wanted to check the meat and find Mule. We went by his house and looked in his window. He wasn't in his room and nobody else in the house was up," Nip said. He looked worried. Nip liked Mule and sort of looked up to him.

"Did you check inside the clubhouse? Did you look in the meat room?" I was a little stung by Nip's concern. I guess I was jealous.

We crawled single file into the clubhouse, Nip first, then me, then Wade. Wade hadn't said anything much, just kept pulling his shirt away from the wounds on his chest and fingering the cuts on his face. When we got inside, Nip lit a candle and held it around the cave-like room. There was nothing in there but our junk, but some of it had been knocked aside, shoved up against the wall, and there was a deep groove down the middle of the sandy floor. The groove led straight from the tunnel to the meat room.

We just stared at it. Then Wade got up the nerve to pull back the boards that covered the entrance to the meat room. As he removed the last board, Nip moved in closer with the candle. As the light edged its way into the dark hole, a huge, naked form flashed out of the blackness and tackled Wade. The two of them fell into the middle of the clubhouse with a thud that made the roof leak some of its sand and dirt. We knew then that Mule was okay. Sometime in the night he had made it back to the clubhouse. Wade had been clobbered by Mule's side of beef.

Four days later we were still eating on that meat. Every day we would spend some time down on the river bank, building fires and trying our hand at cooking it in every possible way. And Mule was the biggest eater, even bigger than Wade. He would stuff that meat — especially the steaks — into himself until he could hardly breathe. The juices ran out of the corner of his mouth. Gulping sounds accentuated his chews. Sometimes, when all of us were eating at the same time, we created a kind of music out of the sounds we made, a sort of rhythm of gulps, belches, smacking, chewing, ripping, hiccuping, snorting and farting. Sounds seemed to blast from every opening in our bodies as the meat slid down our throats.

The four of us ate meat until we literally were sick at the sight of it, and even so we hardly made a dent in the pile. We got picky, choosy about what we would eat. We fished through the packages for choice pieces, for spicy sausages and thick strips of bacon, tiny little round things of tender beef, the ribs that hung together in slabs, anything we could drive a stick through and hold over the fire, anything that we knew would be tender and juicy.

Nip found some pieces of liver wrapped in with some other cuts, and he was about to throw them into the river when he suddenly changed his mind. He got a piece of old rope out of the clubhouse. He found some sort of stringy, springy tree right at the edge of the water, climbed it until it bent toward the bank, then used the rope to tie the top of it to a small stump. He took the liver and carefully placed it on the top of the bent tree, making sure that the liver was properly balanced. Then he cut the rope. The tree swooshed upward and the liver was launched far out over the river, the bloody mass sailing into the bright air and gaining altitude as it headed toward Kentucky. It disappeared into some trees on the Kentucky side and we could hear it breaking small branches. A liver bomb. We talked about how some Kentucky pig fucker would be walking along a path over there and would get hit smack in the face with a load of liver. He would have a hell of a time explaining that! We laughed until we almost threw up.

Mule kept hacking away at the side of beef. Wade poked through everything, toasting a tidbit here, selecting a morsel there. We felt like Robin Hood just after he had slaughtered one of the king's deer. We also began to feel pretty sick.

We were always too filthy for anyone to notice the new juice stains on our clothes, but, just the same, we were pretty careful around town. We didn't know what would happen when the driver missed all that meat. We thought for sure that he'd notice the loss when he got to Tyler's store, but we never found out. The next time the truck came through it was a different driver — we heard Tyler ask him what happened to the other guy — but he wasn't much for talking, just mumbled something about company orders.

So the great meat robbery went unnoticed: that was hard for us to take — nobody talked about how neat the job was, how smart the robbers were, how they must have been professionals to pull it off like that. Nothing. Not a word. That was really hard to take.

At the end of the first week after we robbed the meat truck the meat began to spoil. Parts of it turned green, other parts just stiff, so we cut them off and threw them in the river or launched them over into Kentucky. Soon, however, the green was spreading too fast for us to keep up with and more meat was going into or over the river than was cooking over the fire. We couldn't eat the good meat fast enough to keep ahead of the rot and in the end at least a third went into the muddy current.

I've thought a lot about that meat and how we stole it. And I've thought a lot about Mule and Nip and Wade sitting on a damp river bank eating rotten meat in the near light of a fast evening. The fire and the smell of the cooking meat are still with me. Years later I saw another meat truck in another town far away. And there was a kid standing there looking at it. And I wondered if he had a couple of buddies and a clubhouse down by the river.

AUTUMN

Chapter 7

I loved autumn, the one season of the year that God seemed to have put there just for the beauty of it. The air was lighter and cleaner and it smelled better. Things in the woods seem to calm down, knowing that they are having the last kind days before the wet and blowy winter slams the lid shut on the tops of the mountains. The hardwoods break out in colors hard to describe. The maple lent a brilliant redness to the mountains as the days grew cooler and the nights began to crisp up. Soon you could see for the first time from ridge to ridge, looking through the bare limbs of the hardwoods where weeks before the brush was so thick you could disappear into the woods without a trace in the space of just a few feet.

But the best thing about autumn was that the school opened again and the teachers came back to Crum.

The first few weeks of school were always the best. There were always some new kids who came in on the busses, kids who for some reason had moved into our hills during the summer and who provided us with some real interest. It was fun to try to figure them out. There would be some pushing and shoving and a couple of fights. Some of the new girls would test Ruby's hold, but that didn't last long. Nobody could replace Ruby. Once that was clear, things would settle down quickly.

The skies in autumn would be that soft blue color that could make anything comfortable and the teachers would be in a good mood, always taking walks around the school grounds during lunch hours. We had been trapped in Crum all summer, but they had just arrived, most of them had never been here before, and they just didn't know yet what it was like to spend a winter in Crum. So some of them liked it, at least for a little while.

And in autumn we could play football and be coached by Aaron Mason. The first year that our school was declared a high school, the county school board told us that we could have a football team. So we had one. We had fourteen players, thirteen second-hand uniforms and twelve pairs of football shoes. When the guy who had the uniform but no shoes had to go into the game, the officials would call time-out so the shoes could be changed. The size of the shoes was no problem. We just got a big pair and they fit most everybody.

Coach Aaron Mason was a small man, almost tiny in fact, but with a body of spring steel and wrists bigger than most people's forearms. He was five-feet-five and probably didn't weigh more than 145 pounds, but he could manhandle the largest player on the squad without half trying. He was so fast with his hands and feet that he could move around you, hitting you on the face and the back of the neck almost at the same time. He would challenge us to race him in the hundred yard dash and would be so far ahead by the time he had covered ninety yards that he would turn around and run backwards the rest of the way. Besides coaching the football team at Crum High School, he also coached basketball — although we didn't have a gym — coached baseball, taught English, social science, history and health and was also assistant principal.

We liked football and we loved Coach Mason but the best thing was it got us out of Crum on at least four or five days each autumn, allowed us to see other people, go to a few other places and poke our noses into a few other situations. To start out on a football trip was the best adventure I can recall. It was the football trip that told me that it was out there — whatever it was. When I was on a bus, my neck used to hurt all the time because I stared so hard out the window. I didn't want to miss anything that went by, didn't want to miss the new faces, the houses I had never seen. Once, in Williamson, I saw a house that had three stories and that was the first time I realized that some people could have as many rooms as they wanted, not just the rooms they needed. And Huntington was the biggest city I had ever visited — it had paved streets, sidewalks, and more than one restaurant. Sometimes, where two streets crossed, there were metal discs in the center of the crossing and people said there were pipes and wires down there.

It was always the trip I remembered, not the game.

When we stopped to eat, Coach Mason would go inside the small restaurant, talk to the owner, then come back out and give us a lecture on how to behave. Those were the only lectures in civilized behavior that we had, and the sessions in the little roadside restaurants were our first introduction to the fact that people could eat without sound effects. We would watch other people as they ate, the way they held their forks, placed their napkins, sipped their coffee. And if anything looked good we would copy it. I sure as hell picked up some funny habits that way.

We always ate whatever we recognized, such as pork chops, brown beans — we called them soup beans — corn bread, fried potatoes and huge glasses of milk. Coach Mason would not let us have coffee and he wouldn't let us eat before the game, so we always stopped on the way home.

On our very first trip we discovered that in most restaurants you could get more bread and butter if you asked for it. Soon we were pounding down half a loaf and half a pound of butter apiece. Most of the restaurants would also give you all the iced tea you wanted and we poured gallons down our throats.

I loved Coach Mason. He knew about books and he knew about games and he could tell you about the battle of Gettysburg. He lived in Crum all year and in the fall he would go hunting and once I got to go with him. He carried a big 12-guage shotgun and when the damn thing went off it made me shake with fear. I was never ready for that gun to go off, mainly because Aaron was so fast. When he saw a squirrel or rabbit, the gun was nothing but a blur and then it would go off, the thunder of it thumping into my body and making the woods shake. I loved it. His wife, Martha, would always cook whatever Aaron brought home, and they would invite me to stay and eat with them. Martha was beautiful and gracious and she could fry squirrel better than anybody.

After football practice, when I had no place to go except back to my shed, I would go to the Masons' house. They would let me sit around and read the newspapers that Aaron had mailed to him from Huntington. Martha could play the organ and she could draw, and she would explain music and art. They would talk with me and give me small jobs to do. They had no kids and I think that sometimes they pretended that I belonged there. Once, I know, they talked about my moving in with them, about my leaving my shed on the back of the house on the side of the holler and coming to stay with them. I would eat at their table and sleep in their house. I would draw water from their well. But they never talked to me about it. And I was thankful for that. I don't know what I would have done if they had.

I'll find them again someday, and I'll tell them that I love them. Aaron will probably make me run ten laps.

Chapter 8

One of the first things you noticed about Benny Musser was that he liked to play with his dick. I never knew of any other dick he played with, but he surely did put some miles on his own.

I guess Benny had been around from the day I was born, and he had always looked the same. He was one of those skinny, short little kids who never seem to change. He had brown eyes and stringy, brown hair that seemed to be always too long, but never got any longer. I don't know if he cut it or if it just stopped growing, but I never knew Benny when his hair looked like anyone had touched it.

And Benny was dirty. He didn't have just ordinary dirt, the kind of dirt that you can wash off with a good scrubbing or two. The dirt started out on his skin, a layer of grime that never came off and eventually hardened into something like a protective coating. Ruby said that her mother said that Benny hadn't been born in a house, that he had been born in a field where his mother was working. She said that Benny's mother had just squatted and dropped him into the dirt, and that the dirt never, ever, would come off. Maybe Ruby's mother was right. Even when Benny came to school wearing a clean shirt, which was rare, the shirt didn't make up for the fact that his skin was not like other skin.

The dirt oozed into Benny's mind and lodged there. It became part of his thinking, part of his way of life. And his dirty little mind worked differently from everyone else's. When Benny thought about anything, it seemed to come out dirty. And sort of dumb. I remember his dumbness from the first year I spent in Crum and from every year after that. In most ways, Benny was the dumbest kid I ever knew, but he always got promoted because no teacher could stand the thought of having him around for more than one year. I remember a first-grade teacher going to the back of the room where Benny was sitting, dick in hand, staring out the window. She got pretty upset about the whole thing and she took a ruler and swatted him. She meant to hit him on the wrist, but just as she swung the ruler Benny turned to one side and the ruler smacked him on the dick. He yelled, leaped over backwards and crashed into the wall behind him. By the time he got untangled the whole class had gathered around to see what the devil was going on and there was Benny, both hands clutching his little dick, screaming his head off.

As Benny got older he became less and less cautious about where he played with his dick. His favorite game was to whip out his tool in the back of the classroom and pump hell out of it. Everyone in class, except the teacher, knew what was going on, and everyone's concentration was on that and that alone. The teacher, of course, thought she had everyone's attention.

Benny always sat in the back of the class. Besides making it harder for the teacher to spot him, it gave him a tactical advantage. From the back of the room Benny would chew some paper into a spitball, flip it into the back of the neck of anyone he chose, then flash his dick when the kid turned around. He especially liked to flash it at the girls, but most of them were on to him and wouldn't turn around and look if they thought Benny had his dick out. Not in public, anyway.

Actually, the girls were fascinated by Benny's dick. As he had gotten older, it had gotten bigger, and he probably had the biggest in school. We all said, in our own defense, that it had gotten that big because he was always exercising it, but, for whatever reason, Benny had one hell of a tool on him and the girls — if they thought they could sneak a look without getting caught — could hardly keep their eyes off it.

In spite of everything, Benny never got close to getting laid. And the reason was, frankly, because he was an ugly, unpleasant little runt, his clothes stiff from last month's dirt, the rims of his nostrils caked with grime after long sessions of nose picking with dirty fingers. On rare occasions a girl might let Benny feel her up in return for his flashing his dick but it never went beyond that.

Elvira Prince was a good example. She was sort of the step-daughter of Constable Clyde Prince. Clyde had been married before, to a woman who already had a daughter, Elvira. Clyde's wife ran off and left him with the girl, and Clyde had no choice but to keep her around. Then Clyde married Genna, who was only sixteen at the time. Elvira was pretty and smart. And for some reason she was a tremendous prick-teaser. If there was a better prick-teaser than Ruby, it was Elvira. But there was one major difference between them; Elvira would fuck too, fuck everybody but Benny and that almost drove him crazy, knowing that he was the only guy in school she was saying no to.

Elvira would make trades with Benny, and Benny kept taking the deals, thinking that maybe someday Elvira would trade him the real thing if only he kept at it long enough. Once Elvira traded Benny a five-second feel to get Benny to stick his dick into home economics class. The entire class was girls and Elvira seemed to think that it would be funny. And so did Benny. And besides, to get a hand under Elvira's dress, Benny would do anything. And so he did it. When the girls noticed the dick sticking through the partially opened door they recognized it immediately, even though they couldn't see Benny. They sat for a while, quietly staring. Mrs. Fry, the home economics teacher, droned on about the usefulness of a double boiler to the young housewife, until she noticed that all eyes were on the door, riveted there as surely as if they had been fixed that way from birth. Mrs. Fry turned to see the huge, red whang sticking through the crack. She stared quietly for a few seconds, then seemed to realize what she was looking at. Her scream was heard all the way out on the football field, and to Benny it came as a hell of a shock. He jerked his dick back through the doorway, trying to return it to his pants. Mrs. Fry screamed again, this time rushing the door as she yelled. Benny was still standing directly behind the door and as Mrs. Fry attempted to throw it open she knocked Benny ass over ear lobes against the wall on the other side of the hallway. By this time, Benny had figured out that getting his tool back inside his pants was not quite as important as getting himself the hell out of there and he beat it down the hallway and out of sight, his dick flapping as he ran.

Despite Mrs. Fry's questioning, none of the girls in home economics was willing to admit that she recognized a dick when she couldn't see its owner, so Benny got away. That afternoon after school, Elvira let him feel her crotch. She made him feel it through her pants and that made Benny a little mad, but it was better than no feel at all. And it was as close as he had gotten, though he would do better.

One day in late autumn we were sitting on the steps out in front of the school, doing nothing, looking out across the football field, watching the wind whip the leaves on the tops of the trees on the far ridges. School was out for the day and most of the buses had already gone, but there was about a dozen of us sitting there, not quite ready to go home. As always, Benny had his hand rammed down inside his pants, playing with himself. It was almost time for the daily Greyhound to stop in Crum, and we were just waiting to see it. It was something to do.

Elvira called Benny over and the two of them walked off a little way. They talked for a while, and I could see Benny didn't want any part of it. We all knew about Elvira making trades with Benny, but this time, for some reason, Benny had turned her down.

"Look, Benny, why don't you want to do it?" Elvira sounded irritated and a little unsure of herself. "I'll make it fifteen seconds."

"She-it no!" Benny almost shouted. He always made shit into two syllables. "She-it no, I ain't goin' to do it, not even for fifteen seconds!" Benny sounded as though his pride were hurt, as though he had been offered too small a payment for something he felt was more valuable. Elvira began to squirm a little. Everyone knew Benny had said no.

"Shit, Benny, I offered you fifteen seconds, and a real feel, too, inside the pants. If you think you're going to get a fuck, you got another think coming!" Elvira's face began to get a little red as she talked. She had decided to discuss the trade openly because she wanted everyone to know she wasn't going to give Benny a lay. That would be too much.

Benny turned to Mule. "Hey, Mule, Elly wants to trade me a fifteen-second feel inside her pants if'n I'll go over to the bus stop like I want to catch the bus. Then when the bus stops she wants me to climb up the steps and pull out my dick and wave it at the passengers. She-it fire, man, that bus driver'll kill my ass if'n he gets his hands on me! And that's worth more'n any fifteen-second feel, even inside the pants!"

We gathered tightly around Mule, Benny and Elvira. We were all part of the negotiations now.

"Well, she-it, Mule, ain't it worth more'n that?"

"Look," Mule said to me, "you get Benny and find out what he wants for the trade and I'll get Elly and see what she's willing to give. Man, I'd sure like to see Benny fling his tool on that bus! We just got to do it!"

"Come on, Benny, you know Elly ain't going to give you no real pussy. Now what is it you want in trade?" I said to Benny when I got him alone.

"She-it, man, I want somethin' more'n a feel! She's just got to give me somethin' more'n another goddamn feel! I'll take whatever it is, only it's got to be more'n a goddamn feel!"

Mule and Elly were also talking quietly a little distance from the group. Mule reached out and gently rubbed Elvira's hip as they talked. Elly saw that Benny and I were watching, so she turned slightly, allowing Mule's hand to come to rest on her crotch. Not one to miss an opportunity, Mule began to rub that, too, just so Benny could see.

Mule came back to Benny and me.

"Benny," he said, "Elly is willing to raise her trade some, but she wants to talk private about it."

Benny practically ran to where Elvira was waiting, and we could see them talking. Benny reached out to rub her, but Elly pushed his hand away. She wasn't going to give Benny anything that he didn't trade for. They talked some more and finally Benny just shook his head and folded his arms across his chest. Whatever the increased trade was, he wasn't having any of this deal, either. Elvira began to get a little mad. If we waited too much longer the bus would arrive and be gone, Benny would have refused Elly's offer, and Elvira's reputation would have taken a terrific beating.

They talked some more, both of them, and finally Benny unfolded his arms. Elvira's face was flaming red. It was clear an agreement had been reached.

"Okay," Benny said, "I'll flash it."

We waited for more.

Finally, I said, "What's the trade, Benny? What are you getting for it?"

"Yeah," Mule said, "shit, man, what's the trade?"

Benny just stood there, looking at Elvira. "Well, I agreed not to tell, only I also agreed to tell you that it ain't fuckin'. I ain't gettin' to fuck Elly."

"That's for damn sure," Elly said quickly.

Mule jumped in. "Hell, Benny, then what's the deal? Come on, man, tell us! How do we know you've been paid off if we don't know the deal?"

Benny seemed to be stuck for an answer. If we didn't know for sure how he was to be paid off, what he would receive in trade, there really wouldn't be any use in Benny sticking his dick out at the passengers. This deal was too big to take Benny's word.

"Hey, Benny," I said, "how about telling just one of us? Then we know that you made a good trade and can back you up with the others." Benny looked at me and then at Elly. She knew that something would have to be done if she was to prove that she had paid off but she didn't like the idea. She pulled Benny off to one side and they talked again. Finally, they came back.

Benny looked at me. "Okay, here's what we'll do. I'll flash it at the bus, then you and Mule can watch me get paid. Nobody else or Elvira won't trade. Just you and Mule. You can tell the others about it, but they can't watch. It'll be tomorrow, after school."

From where we had been sitting on the steps of the school, we could see the little store that served as the town's only bus stop. It was across the football field, across the railroad tracks, tucked in between the tracks and the narrow, two-lane highway. There was just enough room for the bus to pull off the pavement without hitting the store.

We started toward the store, trying to look as though we were just messing around, not going any place in particular. We settled down at the far end of the building on a small grassy knoll where kids sat when they came to the store to buy candy bars and soda pop. Downriver, the road curved away toward the left and then went up a small rise. When the bus topped that rise we would be able to see it from where we were sitting. Our plan was to hunker down behind the knoll and watch Benny in action.

"Here it comes! Oh, God, Benny, here it comes! Get ready, Benny!" Ruby yelled. The silver of the bus reflected sparkling light out into the valley.

I could hardly believe my ears — even Ruby was excited.

Benny borrowed Wade Holbrook's baseball cap and my jacket, my best Levi jacket. It had been in the river four or five times, and, last year, had gotten caught on the back bumper of Mean Rafe Hensley's pickup truck and dragged halfway to the beer garden at the top of the mountain. I figured it was nearly broken in.

Benny pulled the cap down over his eyes and rolled up the jacket under his arm, like a traveling bundle. He stepped out in front of the little store and waited, listening to the sound of the bus pushing its way up the river valley.

When it came into sight, Benny hitched his bundle up and held up his hand. For a while it looked as though the bus might not stop. Benny was such a little runt that he really didn't look too serious standing out there. But at the last moment we could hear the air brakes and the sounds of the driver gearing down and we knew it was going to come off.

The bus stopped so close Benny couldn't see the driver through the huge door. Some passengers looked out the window at the small figure in the faded red baseball cap, waiting patiently to get on. The driver took his time, but he finally opened the door. Benny wasn't too anxious to look the driver straight in the eye and kept his face pointed toward the ground as though he might be a little frightened at the prospect of actually getting on the mammoth machine.

The driver shoved on his lever, rattling the door a little, letting Benny know that he didn't have all day to wait for some kid from Crum to get on the bus.

"Boy, you goin' to get on this bus, or what?"

Benny climbed on board. He shoved his hand in his pocket

and pulled out a small piece of paper, shoved it toward the bus driver. As the driver reached for it, Benny let it slip and it fluttered toward the floor of the bus at the driver's feet. The driver bent over for it.

Benny whirled and faced the passengers down the aisle. He ripped open the buttons on his jeans and in one smooth motion reached inside and pulled out his dick, whipping it straight down the aisle.

"Hey!" he shouted, "FUCK YOU!"

Somewhere deep inside the bus a woman screamed and a man began to curse and shout. The driver froze double reaching for the paper, stunned by what was happening. Then a lot of things began to happen at once. The driver came to and made a grab for Benny, missed, and Benny jumped into the front seat of the bus, his tool flapping in all directions. The driver grabbed the door handle and yanked the door shut, intent on trapping Benny inside. But Benny was a quick runt and he was over the handrail, down into the stairwell and out the door at the last second. He leaped straight out the door, hitting the ground several feet beyond the bus, and running all the way. The little sonofabitch had Wade's hat on but he had dropped my jacket inside. I had to hand it to him, though -- that bit with the scrap of paper was really something.

The bus door burst open again almost at once and the driver came roaring full blast down the steps with a look of absolute madness on his face. Bus drivers are held responsible for everything that happens on their buses, and some little ugly fart of a kid had insulted his entire load of passengers and he goddamn well wasn't going to get away with it.

When Benny shot out of the bus he ran straight toward us, then, at the last minute realizing what he was doing, made a sharp turn and cut behind the store, heading for a field about fifty yards away. The driver followed, came within five yards and in full sight of us, but was too hell-bent on Benny to notice. The field was full of weeds, mature and brittle in the autumn sun, and we could hear the two of them crashing their way through towards the river.

As soon as they were out of sight, Mule and I looked at each other and each knew what the other was thinking. Benny had started it and now we wanted in. Both of us started to unbutton our pants. We had only taken a few steps when a huge man appeared at the bus doorway and began yelling at us, his gravel voice slamming into our faces. He shook his fist and cursed and looked like he'd chase us if we took another step. In any case, any chance of actually getting on the damn bus was shot, so we settled for yelling "FUCK YOU!", waving our dicks wildly in the direction of the bus in general, and then getting the hell out of there. The other kids jumped up, everybody yelling "FUCK YOU!" and everybody running off in all directions.

We knew that Benny would probably sleep out in the little barn behind his house that night, just in case they came looking for him. Benny's house sat on a flat at the top of the river bank, on the upriver end of town. The house leaned a little toward the river and it was so small that Benny didn't like sleeping inside. Besides, he didn't have a bedroom. Benny's father had cut out a long time ago and his mother slept in the only bedroom. Benny had to sleep on the floor of the room that was both the living room and the kitchen. So he preferred the barn — although it was a little crowded since we still hadn't gotten rid of our pile of scrap iron.

Later, Mule came over to my sleeping shed and we stayed up most of the night, talking about Benny and his stunt and the woman who had screamed and about the next day when we knew we would see the payoff. It was a great night. Almost better than Christmas.

In school the next day Benny didn't touch himself even once. He was saving up. Elvira looked pleased with herself, since she had been the cause of yesterday's excitement. The word got around pretty quickly and Elly became some sort of heroine-for-the-day with a bunch of guys following her around. The other girls would look at her and you could almost hear them wondering if Benny would have gone to such lengths for them.

It was a long day. We were going to have to sneak away after school, otherwise too many kids would try to get a look at the payoff. So during the day we worked out a plan. When classes let out, Mule and Benny sauntered off in the direction of the bus stop, Elly headed out behind the school toward the huge outhouses, and I just simply started for my house, upriver from the school. A bunch of kids watched us but we didn't seem to be going anywhere together. As soon as they could, Benny and Mule cut through the weed field that Benny had used to escape from the bus driver, I cut back through the old cemetery just above the school, and Elvira just kept going, past the outhouses and over the river bank, down on the sandy flat beside the river and into the cane field.

We met at the end of the cane field. Whoever had planted the cane had never harvested it, and the stalks were dead now, leaning at all angles. Elvira was already there when I arrived. She seemed a little nervous and we talked for a while, waiting for Benny and Mule. She shifted from one foot to the other, looking up and down the river bank, breathing in sharp little bursts of air. I stood looking at her breasts rise and fall from the breathing. After a few minutes I put one arm around her, then began rubbing a breast with my other hand. The breasts rose and fell, rose and fell under my hand. I ran my hand down and then up under her skirt, and then down under her underpants. As I squeezed her cheeks she turned sideways, forcing my hand to slide around her hip. I began to have thoughts about taking her back into the cane field as she spread her legs. Then we both sort of folded down onto the sand — when suddenly Benny popped out of the cane field.

"No! No! That ain't right! It's my turn! It's my payoff, you sonofabitch!"

He tackled me from the side, jabbing my hard-on into the sand. I thought I had broken it. I threw myself over on my back, grabbed Benny's squirming, fighting, little body and flipped him off me.

"Okay, Benny, okay, I was just getting it warmed up for you!" I yelled into his ear. "Now cut it out and I'll let you go, you little bastard!"

Benny sat up and looked at Elvira. "Okay," he said, "let's us do it."

He got to his knees, moved over to Elly and reached carefully up under her dress and took hold of her panties, sliding them slowly down her legs. Mule sat down on the sand so he could get a better view.

Elly spread her legs a little and squatted on the sand, hiking her skirt up. Benny took out his dick and squatted on the sand in front of her. When he squatted, his tool disappeared back inside his pants, so he stood up and tried again. When it disappeared again, he stood up and took off his pants. He wasn't wearing any undershorts — none of us did. All Elly could do was stare. Benny squatted again and reached between Elly's legs.

"Come around here, come around here so you can see!" Benny was saying, and it took a few seconds for us to realize that he was talking to us. We moved around and looked up Benny's arm to where his fist all but disappeared into Elly. He was working the fist slowly back and forth.

"Okay, now take it," Benny said, and Elly reached over and wrapped her fingers around his tool and started to work it back and forth with a push-pulling motion.

"Harder!" Benny blurted out, and Elly drove her hand back and forth along the shaft until I thought Benny's balls would fly off at the roots.

"Now," he said, "do the other thing!"

Hell, it was almost impossible for them to stay squatted down like that and keep their feet, the way they were rocking each other back and forth. Mule and I looked at each other. What other thing could they do from that position?

Then Elvira started to pee. Slowly, gently, to make it last, she released the water out onto Benny's hand, his hand still shoved far up inside her, the water filling his palm and flowing in a warm stream across his wrist, dropping to the ground. Some of the pungent liquid followed his arm back to his elbow and then fell to the sand, making little dripping sounds. All of a sudden he grunted and shot a glob of sperm into the air in a small arc and down onto the ground. It was covered immediately with sand.

Benny was on the verge of passing out. He sat back on the sand, complete satisfaction on his face. Elvira got up, put on her panties, looked at Mule and me for a couple of seconds, then turned and walked down the river bank, into the cane field and out of sight. A few minutes later we could see her topping the bank on the way home.

Benny was still sitting there, the urine drying on his arm. His soft tool dripped on the ground and picked up grains of sand in the process. Mule and I didn't know what to do, so we just walked off. I have to admit, Mule and I thought and felt differently about Benny after that. Not that we felt any better about him, you understand. We still thought he was dumb and filthy, but somehow we had to admit he was one up on us. A lot had happened just because he was dumb and filthy. It made us think.

And I never did get my jacket back. Somebody said it was over at the bus stop, that the driver had thrown it off before he drove away, but I never had the guts to go and ask for it.

Chapter 9

On Halloween all hell seemed to break loose in Crum. Lug nuts were taken off wheels of cars, dogs were tied in the middle of the railroad track, cats were turpentined and turned loose in the beer garden, and one year somebody set fire to a hundred and two individual fodder shocks in the field that belonged to Mule's dad, Herschel. The fire almost reached Herschel's barn, which would have made the whole thing a lot more serious. You don't burn barns in Appalachia without starting the sort of trouble that can last for years, for decades.

On Halloween I looked forward to doing all the things I couldn't do the rest of the year, because the rest of the year everyone would know that I was always the one doing them and I would get caught. Or at least blamed. But I could do them on Halloween because everybody else was doing them too and they couldn't catch all of us.

One Halloween I came home long after midnight and stepped up on the porch that ran along the side of the house, all the way around from the front to the back where my sleeping shed was. I was walking carefully around when I heard a knock at the front door. I ran back around the porch to see who the hell was banging on the door at that hour, and there was something — it looked like a paper bag — burning on the porch in front of the door. I stomped on the flames, stomped on them over and over until they were completely out. I was feeling pretty good about the whole thing, congratulating myself on saving the house when Oscar opened the door and shone a lantern out on the porch, trying to see what the hell all the noise was about. At about the time I began to smell something funny. It was suddenly pretty obvious what had happened. The burning paper bag had been full of shit. I had stomped shit all over the porch, all over me, and all over the front wall of the house. Whoever had done the thing had waited until I had come home, had waited until he knew it was me, and then had lit the bag and left it on the porch, just for me. There was a lot of shit in that bag. And it was fresh.

I went around back to my shed and stood outside the door and took off all my clothes. My pants were covered and, handling them carefully, I threw them out into the darkness. Naked, I went out to the well and drew a bucket of cold, hard water. I scrubbed my legs and feet, rubbing them first with a brush and then with my hands. The water was so cold I numbed myself. Mattie came out and laughed at me standing there in the dark, shaking and naked. She had an old sheet and she threw it over me and I rubbed my body until I was clean and dry.

I had no way to prove who threw that bag of shit, but I knew, somewhere in my gut, that it was Ethan Piney. And knowing, really knowing, that it was Ethan made my stomach burn. Every time I saw Ethan after that, my stomach burned. And, of course, somehow it got around the school that I had fallen for the oldest Halloween trick known, stomping on a bag of shit. And, since I sure as hell didn't tell anyone, it had to have been Ethan who was doing the telling.

Actually, the whole thing was pretty funny. Ruby sure thought it was. And for a week after that Mule carried little brown paper bags around in his pocket. Every time he saw me coming down the hallway of the school, he'd pull one out, throw it on the floor, and stomp on it. The fucker thought that was really funny. I used to wonder about Mule when he did things like that. I mean, he was supposed to be my friend, maybe my best friend. And then he would do something like that.

Halloween drew a special madness from the people in Crum. The ones who went out and participated in the madness were one type, but the ones who stayed at home and made a big fuss over defending their houses against the forces of evil and madness, well, they were quite another. And Reverend Herman Piney was one of those.

Herman Piney was self-ordained. He also was as tall as Tyler Wilson, twice as wide, fat as an autumn pig, and meaner than hell. And to top it all off, of course, he was Ethan Piney's father. Herman conducted revival services only because he had learned the hard way what most Appalachian preachers were taught by the church — when your knowledge of religion runs out, start to shout. That gets home to them every time, and, besides that, no one can wonder what you've said if you never stop shouting long enough for them to ask questions. That was Herman Piney's technique, just to shout the congregation into abject guilt, then line 'em up at the dipping trough and run 'em through the water. A year later he would do it all over again, for surely they had sinned again.

The parson would scream from the pulpit, the sweat running freely from his rolls of fat, his rantings punctuated at proper intervals by an "Amen!" from his wife, who always sat in a straight-back chair off to the side. If there was anyone in town who was fatter than the parson, it was the parson's wife. Her enormous cheeks hung over the sides of the chair, and when she gave out with an "Amen!" the rolls of fat would start quivering from her stomach and spread up and down at the same time, flowing down to her knees and up to her mountainous breasts. The breasts would quiver last, vibrating gently. When we were younger, no one ever had to make us go to church. We went willingly, just to see Mrs. Piney shake and vibrate. Once, during a particularly vigorous Amen!, one of her tits, the right one I think, just simply escaped. It climbed out and popped loose underneath the top of her dress, expanding and breathing and moving as she moved. She knew it had gotten loose, of course, but there was nothing she could do about it. It was the only time I can remember liking church.

Preacher Piney was just plain mean, and I used to wonder why the people of Crum put up with him. But in a town like Crum, you're lucky to get any sort of preacher to spend any time there, and Herman was actually living in Crum full-time. We thought we were lucky. Maybe they even liked him. I know for sure that they were scared of him.

Preacher Piney measured his success by the number of people he baptized. Mostly in West Virginia people got baptized by being dunked in some creek somewhere, but the only stream around Crum deep enough to baptize anyone in was the Tug River, and adults just wouldn't let themselves be dunked in that water. So Herman got himself a water tank, the kind they put out to water the cows, and he installed it in the back of the church, high up on a platform where everybody could see as he dunked the sinners. There were curtains on each side of the tank and he would take the sinners up there, one at a time, and they would change into a white robe, ready to be dunked. He baptized a lot of people, but I never heard anybody say that the water was ever changed.

Herman loved to baptize women, especially unmarried women, especially the younger girls. As the girls waded into the tank he would start his routine, his voice rising with the thrill of it all, his arm around the girl, pulling her tightly against him. Then he would lay her over on her back, his left hand under her shoulders, his right arm reaching around her waist. As he lowered her down beyond the rim of the tank, he would slide his right arm farther down until he felt the girl sort of floating in the water. Like a flash, he would run his right hand between her legs, spreading them until he could get his hand in her crotch. And Preacher Piney would get himself a handful of paradise.

The Preacher just kept on feeling up the girls, right up until the time he baptized Ruby. One of the things new families did when they moved into town was go down and join the town's only church. So Ruby and her parents did that, joined the church, I mean. On the Sunday that they were going to be baptized, I went down to Ruby's house and walked to church with them. I just wanted to be near Ruby when she was all dressed up like that. I wouldn't go inside the church, but I stood outside and looked in through the window. When it was Ruby's turn to be dunked, she climbed up behind the curtain and put on the robe, then waded into the water. Reverend Piney leaned Ruby back and I saw her disappear below the rim of the tank, and I realized that the other people in the church could not see anything that went on in the water. So they had no idea why Herman Piney suddenly stopped his preaching, began to choke, let go of Ruby and folded up, his huge body disappearing below the rim of the tank as he fell like a whale into the water. He overflowed the tank and the water cascaded over the top. The waterfall thundered out and down from the platform, smashed into the pulpit, and inundated the first rows of the faithful.

Ruby told me about it. She wasn't willing to give Reverend Piney what she wouldn't give me. When Herman had grabbed her by the cunt, she had grabbed him by the balls. And twisted.

Herman Piney was against Halloween. My God, was he against Halloween. A black celebration of the devil, he called it. He was also against smoking, drinking, fornication, lipstick, sports, women wearing pants, gambling, hair dye, farting in church, picking your nose, playing with yourself, and fondling the tits of your neighbor's wife. But he was really against Halloween.

A few weeks after Benny had flashed the Greyhound bus, it was Halloween and a group of us were going around town knocking on doors and yelling about trick or treat and hoping that someone would send us screaming into the night with a load of beans and salt from a shotgun which, as we saw it, would give us reason to come back and remove his porch. And we decided to go to Parson Piney's house, which was located about a third of the way up Beecher's Mountain and looked out over most of the town. The house sat on the brink of the steep hill, the front porch reaching almost exactly to the edge. The parson was proud of the house. It was the highest in town and he liked the feeling of being able to watch over his flock.

On the way to the parson's house, we got to wondering if Ethan would be there. Ethan liked Halloween as much as any of us — as I knew well — but we hadn't seen him all night. We talked about it, then decided that we didn't give a damn if Ethan was there. In fact, it might make the whole thing more fun.

There were twenty of us by the time we got there. The group just grew as it became obvious that we were going to the parson's. When we got there, standing out in front of the porch, everyone was strangely quiet. No one wanted to do the knocking.

Of course it was Benny who stepped up on the small porch and banged on the door. Benny was going to bang on the door three or four times, I guess, at least his fist was in the air after the second bang, but he never got to the third one. The door flew open and fat Parson Piney was standing there with a huge bucket. He let it fly in one smooth motion. The first part of the water struck Benny full in the face, toppling him backwards, tumbling him across the porch and down the steps. I could hear his head hit the porch and steps as he tumbled. He was screaming.

We found out why. The rest of the water came out over us, and that water was hot. Not scalding, mind you, but hot enough to scare hell out of all of us. Several in the group fell back over the edge of the hill. The kids nearest the door turned and ran full into the kids behind them, and most of us just fell down in the confusion.

That's when the parson turned on the real waterworks. An upstairs window flew open and buckets of water began flying from the house, drenching everyone in sight. The parson's wife was up there, working her plump ass to the bone, flailing with all her might and with God on her side, dumping buckets of water on the invaders. And, someone said later, although I never really could see, Ethan was up there, too, handing the water to his mother.

We fell back down the hill and tried to figure out what to do next. It was obvious that this was going to be a long night, and that the challenge had been issued in full knowledge that it would be accepted and returned. The parson was building up enough evil to last through a year's worth of sermons. He could lash out at us, the criminals in the town households, until he got to the point where he had to start shouting again, and by that time he would be mad enough to shout about anything, so we were furnishing the parson with enough shouting material to make his face go red for a month of Sundays. But that didn't matter at the time. All that mattered was what to do about the parson.

We didn't know what else to do except drag our dripping bodies back up the hill and knock on the door again. The parson wasn't anywhere that we could see, and if he wasn't out in plain sight the only way to get him to come out was to knock on his door — again. The thing we absolutely could not do was to interfere with the parson's house in any way — like throwing something through the window — because that would give him reason to shoot at us for real. Sure, we talked a lot about tearing off porches or whatever, but we never did any of that kind of stuff. As I've said, you just didn't mess with a man's house, not really.

We got back to the house and Benny marched up the steps and banged on the door. This time, we weren't packed in quite so tight. If the water treatment came again, a little space would be to our advantage. But we underestimated the parson.

We didn't notice at the time, but the upstairs window was still open. The first paper bag that came out of the darkness floated down in slow motion. It hit Mule Pruitt on the shoulder and burst, and coal cinders and wood ashes wafted over the crowd like the plague. The cinders shot from the bursting bag and sprayed over us, ending up under our shirts and down the backs of our necks. The fine ashes ballooned into the night air and cut off our escape and our breathing at the same time. Another bag followed after the first, and then bag after bag came bombing down on us until the air was too thick to breathe, the earth was gray and we were ghostly white, covered with an acrid layer of fine ash. And most of us had been soaking wet when the whole thing started. The mixture of cinders, ashes and water gave us the look of condemned souls, which I suppose is what Reverend Piney had in mind.

It was back down the hill again, coughing and scratching, rubbing our eyes, pounding each other on the backs and trying not to get the damn stuff inside our pants. But it was no use. The parson had won rounds one and two and there was no way we could change that. Pretty soon we quit trying and just sat there, looking up the hill at the house and wondering in our little minds just what the hell the next step was. The idea of walking away, of course, just never occurred to us.

Then, in the tradition of act first and think later, we went back up the hill. We were standing out in front of the house again, wondering what the parson could possibly think up next and how the hell he would do it to us, whatever it was, when the door crashed open and the parson charged out on the porch. The porch light went on and the parson's wife came out behind him. God, I could tell we were in for something. The parson stood there, Bible in hand, his black coat buttoned all the way up the front, his wife standing behind and slightly to the side of him, a lace shawl draped over her arm. Her mountainous chest began to quiver, even before anybody said anything. It struck me that I had seen all this before, through the window of the parson's church — it was his preaching stance, and I figured we were going to get the full sermon.

He opened his big mouth and the words began to flow. Blessed be ye, he shouted, for ye know not what ye do! Ye shall roast in hell for thine actions and for thine evil tongues — Amen, brother! — and God shall punish you through everlasting life. He raised his Bible — Amen! his wife said from behind him — and waved it us.

The parson was getting it into high gear now and his wife was beginning to Amen! more frequently, and we just stood there, frozen. And just at the top of one of the preacher's wife's loudest Amens!, Benny did it. He had been standing there, on the edge of the group, waiting for the right moment, and when the parson's wife opened her mouth he let fly with an apple that he must have had in his pocket for at least a week. As it flew through the air you could see bits of it break off and spin away; the very rottenness of the thing seemed to propel it. It smacked the parson's wife full in her left ear, bouncing off and spattering the screen door. Her mouth snapped shut and she grabbed her ear, whirling to face the direction from which the apple had come.

The parson was puzzled and fell momentarily silent. He had seen an object fly through the air and he had heard the splatting sound, but he was so wound up in his sermon that he didn't really know what had happened. All he knew was his wife was ready to charge.

At the last second, she halted. She glanced at the parson, saw the puzzled expression on his face and fell instantly to her knees.

"Oh, God," she cried, "I have been stoned by the evil in this place! A stone, a stone, a stone has struck my head and I am in mortal pain!" All the parson heard was "stone", and he saw his wife on her knees screaming in front of a group consolidated unto evil. The parson went raving, screaming, foaming mad.

It was an awesome sight, given that the man was a 270-pound preacher and had God on his side. He hurtled forward and grabbed the first kid he could get his hands on, which happened to be Cyrus Hatfield, a pretty good-sized guy, himself. The parson lifted Cy by his jacket and flung him bodily over the hill. In the faint glow from the porch light I could see Cy rolling end over end, bounding down the hill, his arms flopping and flailing, one of his shoes coming off and popping into the brush. Holy shit! If the parson could handle Cy like that, the rest of us didn't have a chance.

Bodies began to spin off in all directions as he took his holy vengeance. His wife kept on screaming in the background and the pitch of her yelling just drove the parson that much harder. His huge arms swung about madly as he bulldozed his path. And then he got to me. I didn't know what to do. I couldn't figure fast enough to get out of the way and as I tried to make up my mind the parson knocked the hell out of me. His arm struck me full in the chest and I went down, my breath feeling like broken glass in my throat. I lay on the ground, bleary-eyed, watching the carnage above me. As the parson plowed his way to the other edge of the group I could sense that people were trying to get the hell out of there, and if I waited too much longer I might be the only one hanging around waiting for the second coming. But I discovered that I wasn't breathing properly just yet. It took a few more precious seconds to get my lungs back in operation, then I stood up and tried to take a step. And the parson appeared dead center in front of me.

"Repent, sinner! On thy knees, thou disciple of the devil!" He pressed me down with one of his ham-like hands. I felt my knees start to give and I knew that if I hit the ground he would mash me like a bug and I would probably end up telling him that I had seen the light and beg him to save me from the devil in that big cow-dunking pool in the back of his church.

Having made that decision, I came up off the ground and in one smooth motion with all the power I could focus, I smashed the good parson straight in the middle of his fat lips. I felt knuckles meet teeth. He didn't even put his hand to his mouth, and I could see his lips split horizontally and vertically.

The world went silent. The stillness was broken only by the sound of running feet beating it down the hill into the darkness and then to the highway and then across the railroad tracks and among the scattered houses and into the total blackness of the fields beyond.

I picked up a lot of speed on the first stretch down the hill. For a moment, I dreamed I had ended it. Then an enormous, roaring, echoing, bellowing poured down the hill after me and I knew the parson had recovered. He bellowed again and this time the bellow was closer. I grabbed a quick glance over my shoulder to see what the hell was going on. What I saw through the darkness was the parson, his huge bulk in high gear, booming down the hill in hot pursuit, the wrath of God spurring him on, the forces of goodness fueling him.

When I first saw the parson chasing me I thought because he was so big that I could outdistance him easily. As I ran I began to close in on some of the others. I passed them one by one. But I couldn't seem to widen the gap on the parson.

We hit the highway and shot straight across, down the embankment, across the railroad tracks and into the light in front of Luke's restaurant. We pulled up there, puffing and sweating, safe in the light from Luke's front porch, thinking about the cool soda pop inside, only to realize that the parson was already across the railroad tracks and not slowing down at all, and that the blood was running in a steady stream from his mouth, spreading across his chin, down his neck, and staining the white collar that stuck up from inside his black coat.

We ran again, desperation leading to a new tactic. As we rounded the first corner of the restaurant and turned up a long dirt lane to the river, Benny split off and headed across an open field. Benny was gambling. If Parson Piney chased him alone, he was really in for it, because Benny just wasn't the fastest man alive. But Benny was pretty sure that the parson would chase the larger group. And so Benny got away.

Down the lane toward the river we ran before the storm, unable to open the gap between us and the parson. As we approached a house, Wade dived under the porch. Cyrus escaped by means of an open ditch. He meant to leap over it but he didn't make it. In any case the parson didn't stop for him, either, and it began to be pretty clear that no matter how small the group became, as long as I was in it, the parson would follow. He wanted me.

Another hundred yards and it was only Mule Pruitt and me. And the parson. It was going to have to be the river unless we could slip him. Up ahead was a corn field, the tall cornstalks already harvested and standing in fodder shocks like row upon row of Indian teepees. It was a maze, a huge chess board with all the chess pieces standing tall and identical in the moonlight. It was perfect.

Mule and I ran silently now, our shoes making crunching noises on the dirt lane. I was openly tiring and Mule was running with an uneven stride, his side cramping up and one of his legs pulling up short.

"The corn field, Mule!" I gasped.

"Yeah, in the shocks!"

We turned on a last burst of speed and began to pull away from the parson. We were fifty yards ahead when we burst into the corn field. Mule and I hit the field at full bore, went in about three rows, then split up, Mule running upriver, me running down. We dived into fodder shocks, pulling the cornstalks closed behind us.

Fodder shocks, no matter what they look like on the outside, have little or no room inside. I had to thrash around a lot to make a little space where I could crouch down in the center of the shock. I hunkered down there in my cornstalk cell, trying not to move, clamping my hand over my mouth and nose to cut down my gasping. Even so my chest heaved and rustled the stalks and I thought I was going to throw up.

I also thought we were safe. With two or three hundred identical shocks standing in one field, there wasn't much chance of the parson flushing us out, even in the bright moonlight. Not unless he was about to do a shock-to-shock check.

Over the beat of my heart and the rasping of my breath I heard the parson arrive in the field, his heavy feet betraying his exertion, his pace uneven, his tread sloppy. He stopped dead and then there was only silence.

I didn't make a sound. I waited, shaking, trying not to rattle any of the cornstalks, knowing that a tiny rustle would scream to the parson "Here I am, come and stomp hell out of me." If we had to run again, I didn't think Mule would make it. I listened and I listened but the world was silent. Out there in the moonlight a great hulk of a God-swearing preacher was waiting to beat my ass into a pulp, but I didn't know what to do beyond what I was doing — just trying not to rattle the cornstalks.

I first heard the sound from about twenty yards away. It was a punching noise, sharp and rustly, a sound you might make by slamming your fist into a sack of beans. It was followed by another identical sound, a few seconds after the first. Then, just a bit later, the two sounds were repeated, and then again, and again.

I had to have a look, I couldn't help it. I had to see what the hell was going on out there, see what was working its way, eating its way, toward my fodder shock. It took about a million years, but I finally got a small hole made in the side of the fodder shock by pushing my arm through in front of my face, carefully pressing each stalk aside long enough to get a peek. I put my eye to the rough hole and peered out into the soft moonlight.

At least as far as three or four fodder shocks down my row there was nothing there. The sound was coming from that direction, but there was nothing to see. I'd held my breath for about five minutes so I inhaled a long gulp of air and pushed another hole in the fodder shock, in the meantime keeping my eye glued to the first one. Before I got my arm all the way through, I saw movement down between the rows. It looked like something jerking up and down, but in the dim light it was hard to be sure. I heard the punching sound again, and this time I was sure of what I saw. It was an arm and on the end of the arm was a hand and the hand was grasping a hoe down by the blade and was thrusting the handle like a lance into the fodder shocks, twice, savagely into each shock. If you happened to be hiding in that fodder shock it would knock hell out of you.

It was time to cut out. The parson was working in my direction, and I guessed if he hit pay dirt with the hoe handle he would turn the hoe around and beat the crap out of the fodder shock — and whoever was in it — with the blade of the hoe. He was getting close, working now in my row. Suddenly, he rammed the hoe into the shock next to mine.

I burst out, screaming my head off, and hurling cornstalks at the parson's terrified face. I saw him almost fall over backwards, catch himself, squat quickly, grab at his ass with both hands, then recover and come up running. I couldn't be sure, but I think the parson had shit his pants. I took off down my row of fodder shocks, heading for the river. I kept on screaming for about the first twenty yards to let Mule know my direction. And the chase was on again.

I was running again and the parson wasn't far behind and I knew that this time I might as well just head for the river and be done with it. I wasn't particularly eager for a swim in the night, but I didn't think the parson was either and it was fast becoming my only hope. The fat sonofabitch just kept coming on.

I hit the edge of the corn field and turned down a dirt offshoot toward the river. The lane ended in the front yard of Homer Wiley, a crusty old man who lived alone at the top of the river bank and raised chickens. I could run around his house and his chicken yard and get down to the river that way, or I could take a shortcut by turning in between his house and his chicken yard, a little pathway about three feet wide. We often cut through there on the way to the river, running a stick along the chicken wire and stirring up Homer's chickens and getting Homer so damn mad he'd come out with a shotgun.

I thanked God for the shortcut this time, because I felt sure that the parson didn't know it was there. I ran along the house to the chicken yard, then made a snappy turn into the shortcut, barreling myself down between the house and the chicken fence at full tilt. I had made my turn and built my speed back up with three or four good strides when I crashed headlong into something across the pathway. That old bastard Homer had built a fence across our shortcut.

He had used chicken wire to seal it off and my face had crashed into the stuff with enough force to cut a network of lines from my forehead to my chin. I went down for good. I wouldn't be running again.

I felt around my feet, trying to find a stick, a rock, anything that I could use to defend myself. There was nothing. My back against the sealed-off pathway, I waited. If the parson turned down the shortcut, I would dive at his feet and hope to knock him down, take him out cold. The pounding sounds of his running grew near, a great slapping that broadcast how tired he was, resounding along the side of Homer Wiley's house, heading toward the shortcut.

He went by. He just ran by it. He didn't even slow down. He ran on into the darkness, heading down to the river bank, chasing something that wasn't there, his great black bulk passing like a locomotive without a train. As soon as I was positive that the sound of his footsteps was actually receding into the night, that he wasn't faking the direction he had taken, I eased out of the shortcut and limped off in the other direction. The air smelled faintly of shit. The blood was making my face sticky with new little lines of red, and my legs were not making much sense anymore, but I forced myself into a trot. I looked back once. There were no lights on in Homer Wiley's house.

I got back to the corn field, went across another lane and into an apple orchard. I kept going. I would trot for a few minutes, then stop to listen for sounds of pursuit. There was nothing. I was alone in the darkness. I didn't dare go back to my house. Everyone including the parson knew that I slept in the shed behind the house, and chances are that he would go there as soon as he realized that he had lost me.

In fact, I couldn't go to anybody's house, not at that time of night, and with my face looking like that. So I went to Herschel Pruitt's barn, about half a mile away, climbed in through the hay loft, wrapped myself in a horse blanket, and buried myself in a pile of hay. My face began to swell and scab over, but at least I was warm and dry and the Servant of God was not going to find me. It didn't make it any better that Mule was probably inside the house, curled up in his own bed.

Chapter 10

The vine went high up into the tree, right to the very top, tangling among branches that were out of sight, reaching for the light at the top of the tree and strangling the tree in the process.

The four of us contemplated the vine and the tree as we lay sprawled in a pool of sunlight, stretched out on our backs on a layer of leaves that covered an even softer layer of the duff and moist earth that builds up on forest floors. Nip, Wade, Mule and I were in no hurry. We had no particular place to go. And the last place we wanted to go was back to town. We were hiding out. We were damn good at hiding out. I never knew a kid from Crum who wasn't. None of us had been to school for three days, none of us had been home for four days, and none of us had had a change of clothes for five days. If we didn't do something soon about cleaning ourselves up, the preacher could follow the smell right into the mountains.

When I had awakened in Herschel's barn the morning after Halloween, my face was so swollen that I could hardly open my eyes. The swelling was mostly from the cuts, I knew, and would go away soon, but in the meantime I was almost blind. I crawled out of the horse blanket and tried to squint through a crack in the planks. For all I knew, the preacher was out there with a bunch of friends, ready to torch the barn.

About noon Mule came slithering in, trying not to make any noise. He climbed the ladder into the loft and whistled softly. I can't remember being so glad to see anybody, even if I couldn't see him too clearly. When he saw what I looked like, he sneaked back and got a bucket of water. I took off my shirt and dunked it in the bucket, then used it to soak my face. I told him I was going to hide out. I didn't have to talk Mule into going with me. He was ready. He had gone back to Luke's restaurant last night to see if anybody else was hanging out there, and the parson had showed up again. Mule took off and spent the night on the riverbank. He had no intention of being seen for a while.

"Man," Mule whispered in the dim light of the barn, "you should have seen that preacher when he come back to the restaurant. He was still lookin' fer you. Said that it didn't really make any difference if he caught you or not, that God had seen you hit his wife with a big rock, and what he would do to you wouldn't be nothin' compared to what he had asked God to do. Then the sonofabitch made a run at me, tried to corner me at the back of the restaurant. Jesus, did he stink! So I took off and stayed out all night. Hell, man, I thought about comin' back to this here barn, but I thought it'd be the first place that preacher would look."

"Yeah, I guess you're right. Only I wasn't thinking too much last night. You seen anybody this mornin'? Where the hell was Ethan last night?"

"I ain't seen nobody, and not Ethan, neither. They said that Ethan was down at the church all night but I don't believe that bullshit. They said the preacher sent him down there before dark yesterday to keep watch on the place, make sure nobody did anything, broke in, or anything like that. Fuck that. I think Ethan was upstairs, throwing that shit down on us."

"You think the parson's goin' to keep lookin' fer me?"

"Shit, man, he's goin' to keep lookin' fer *anybody* until he finds *somebody* that he can wring out fer hittin' his wife. He's told everybody in town that you're the one what did it. But he'll settle fer ketchin' anybody. And we're all goin' to git our asses kicked unless we can git whoever it was that hit his wife to 'fess up."

"That was Benny."

"Yeah, I know."

"And Benny ain't ever goin' to admit what he did."

"Yeah, I know."

"Shit. I guess we're in some fuckin' trouble."

"Yeah, I know."

"So, let's get the shit out'a here."

And we did.

We Gathered up odds and ends that we might need in the woods — mostly stuff like gunny sacks, a hatchet, and a couple of horse blankets. We went out the back of the barn, across a corn field and made our way to the railroad tracks. We used the steep railroad bed to cover us until we got to the culvert underneath the tracks at the edge of town. Once on the other side, we made a break for the woods and the hills. In the hills, we were safe. And in the first fifteen minutes of being in the woods, we ran into Wade and Nip. We were all doing the same thing — hiding out from the preacher. Except for Benny. Where the hell was Benny?

Good swinging vines were hard to find, and when we found this one we thought it was really fine one, so we hacked it loose at the bottom and tested it by pulling and twisting and putting our weight on it. It felt okay. The tree was tall and sort of slender and the vine would give a long way if you really put your weight on it, but it was safe enough. Nip was the lightest, so he tried it first. He took the vine and scrambled up the hill, going for a little height. He faced downhill, grabbing as high up on the vine as he could. He pulled on the vine then, and as he took up the slack he leaped into the air and grabbed the vine even higher before the tree could whip it back. The vine threw Nip out over the hillside in a great, easy arc, pulling him down the slope first, then, as he hit the bottom of the arc, sending him out over the countryside. For a few seconds Nip was king on the end of the vine, no one able to touch him, going where the vine wanted him to go, nothing between him and the sky.

The vine reached the end of the arc and the top of the tree bent a little under Nip's weight. He let go of the vine as his feet hit the ground, ran a couple of steps and stopped. His face was full of the swing, the flight. He didn't say anything to anybody, he just went off to the side and sat down. The vine was okay.

Mule tried it next. He was about forty pounds heavier than Nip. It would be another good test of the vine. He could really swing on vines, that Mule. It seemed okay for us then, so Wade tried it and then it was my turn. I was glad to go last.

After all, if that vine could hold Wade, it could hold anybody. When Wade hit the vine the tree shuddered and bent, but it held and he got a good swing out of it.

I was a little scared out there on the end of the vine just when it reached its highest point. That's when, just for a fraction of a second, you are stopped, hanging on the end of a thread, wondering if it's going to let you down easy or if the thing has made its last swing and is going to drop you straight down and into the brush below. But it didn't and I got back okay. We all took turns then, flying into the edge of the reaches where none of us had been, feeling the air in our noses and ears, enjoying the rush through our chests and hands.

It was Nip's turn again, and then Mule's, and as each of us gained more confidence on the vine we pulled it farther back up the hill before we started our short run. Soon, we were straining at the vine while still standing on the ground, trying to pull it up to a rock that jutted out of the ground far uphill from our swinging tree. Mule tried to get the vine to the rock, and so did I, and each time we got a little closer, and each time the tree gave a little more and the vine stretched. Nip was too light to do much, but then Wade tried again and this time he made it to the rock, holding onto the rock with one hand and the vine with the other as he climbed on top. As he gained the top of the rock and tried to stand up, the tension of the tree pulling on the vine suddenly whipped him off the rock and out into the air. He sailed past us, five feet off the ground and rapidly gaining altitude, on his way to the best swing yet. Wade went so far out he actually grew smaller in the distance and we each silently wished we had been the first. Mule and I decided to help each other to the rock, and to hold each other there until we had a good grip on the vine and were ready to make the swing. We were going for the record.

Mule climbed to the top and I took the vine from Wade and pulled it up the hill. It was almost easy now to reach the rock and I handed the vine to Mule. He took a high grip, squatted a little, then leaped into the air. He started down the hill almost slowly, gracefully, picking up speed in a smooth transition. I climbed on the rock and waited as he came soaring back, tumbling onto the ground several feet in front. We were really getting into it now, really beginning to feel that the swing was more than a vine.

I was ready for it. I grabbed as high up on the vine as I could and jumped, pushing at the rock with all my strength. When I left the rock I knew this was going to be the greatest ride of all. As I swung past the others I could feel the top of the tree giving way, bending farther and farther toward the weight at its end, allowing me to gain more and more speed before I began the ascent. Finally the tree refused to give any more and the sharp resistance made my climb steep and spectacular. The pressure on my hands and arms made me scream with exhilaration and pain. And I rose with the scream, higher into the soft, late afternoon warm air. Just before the top of the swing, just before I reached that point where my return would start, where I would come back to the hillside and the leaves and the soft earth beneath the tree, just before the earth grew large again, the top of the tree spat out branches and leaves and twigs and my vine with a rending, popping, cracking sound, and I was left sailing, still clutching the vine, delirious with fear. The earth was a huge ball and there was no way I could keep from hitting it. I moved through the air in a frozen state, my tense body anticipating impact, my mind taking in all those things that mattered. I wondered at the sudden sharpness of my vision — the green of the grass growing among the trees and bushes, the sky varying from blue to gray, then slightly, fuzzily, red as I crashed through the treetops on my way to earth.

The world was on fire and the fire was liquid and it was all happening inside my head. I tried to get my eyes open, but a weight was pressing on my face and I couldn't make it. Then I realized I was lying on my face and bits and pieces of the earth were plugging my eyes and nose and mouth. Through the roar in my ears I could hear the crashing of brush and I figured that the others were coming to find me. I wanted them to hurry because I couldn't breathe and I didn't know where my arms and hands were and I figured that I was checking out. Dying. Then hands found me and turned me over, hands gouged the earth from my mouth and nose, hands punched and probed and then fell still on my body because I did not move.

But I did move, a little later on. Slowly at first, then more sure of myself. Ten minutes later, so Mule told me, I was sitting up, trying to make my mouth work, and finding bits of leaves and small sticks in there. It was some time before I could walk, but it didn't matter, since no one was really in a hurry to go anywhere. In fact, there was nowhere to go. After all, we were hiding out.

Hiding out was fun but it also got a little scary. It wasn't the hiding out, exactly. It was not knowing what was going on back in town. It was wondering where the preacher was, and what he had done while we were gone. And what he had in mind for us when we got back. We had been in the woods for four days and that was plenty of time for the preacher to cool off or to get even hotter. The problem was, we didn't know which.

While we had been in the woods we had been collecting black walnuts in our gunny sacks, and each of us had about a half-full sack. The walnuts, with their moist hulls and their thick shells, were heavy and about half a sack full was as much as one guy could carry for any distance and about as much weight as the sack could stand. But we always gathered more than we could carry and we would drag the sacks along the ground rather than try to lift them. At least one sack always broke under the strain and all the dark, round nuts would spill along the ground like a cascade of giant, black marbles. And the owner of the sack would always curse and just leave the walnuts lying there, after having wasted a whole day gathering them across five miles of woods.

So we had all the walnuts we could carry, and it was time to go back and try to find out what the hell was going on. And besides, early last summer we had promised Mule's dad, Herschel, that we would trade him some walnuts if we could watch the next pig butchering. Actually, we could have watched the pig butchering anyway, but we knew that if we gave him the walnuts, he would give us the pig's bladder.

And that's why we started back to Crum. At least, that's what we told ourselves. We staggered down the hill, each of us under his own load of walnuts. My legs were only working under protest and my face stung from the old wire cuts and the new bashes that it had taken when it rammed into the ground. I was a mess. With each step my body announced another cut or sore place. When I got to the bottom of the hill I looked back and I could see the tree up there, the top looking no different than I remembered it. For a quick moment that instant of freedom was back in my mind and I could taste the flight again, more than a sip this time. I had had a solid swallow and I thought that probably the swallow was worth the trip.

We walked out on a dusty road and my gunny sack split across the bottom. All my walnuts rolled out onto the dirt.

Chapter 11

Sometime while we were hiding out in the hills Benny arranged for the preacher to be told that I hadn't been the one who hit his wife. I don't know how he did it — it took guts — and I'm sure he didn't talk to the preacher directly, but somehow he let him know it wasn't me. Word also got around town it wasn't a rock that hit the preacher's wife, just an overripe apple, and the preacher had tried to run down some kids who hadn't done anything. Well, not much of anything, anyway. The preacher wound up looking pretty foolish for losing his head and I guess the little detail about his split lip got overlooked too. At least I thought so.

All I know is the preacher wasn't waiting for us when we finally walked back into Crum, dragging our sacks of walnuts. In fact, he wasn't in town. He had taken his fat wife and that pig fucker Ethan and gone on a trip. No one seemed to know where, and I didn't really care. For a time, at least until he cooled off a little more and came back to Crum, I was safe.

Herschel Pruitt always butchered pigs in the fall. All the kids would beg him for the bladders. There were never enough of them to go around but Mule and I always got one because Mule was his son, and because I could trade him a peck basket of walnuts.

Pig bladders were great. You could blow them up and tie them off so they wouldn't leak and then have the damnedest game of crazy football you ever saw. A pig bladder was much lighter and would sail away when you kicked it, carried along by the breeze. Only rarely would a bladder last for two whole football games — they always burst before they rotted.

I wouldn't get a bladder this time, not if I knew Herschel. Sooner or later I would have to tell Herschel my bag of walnuts had burst on the road. No walnuts, no bladder, that was his policy. When I finally got around to dropping by Herschel's barn, they were just getting ready to do the job. The day was perfect, bright and crisp and fresh, and there was no breeze at all. It was just the sort of day to do a little butchering.

There were large kettles of water boiling over open fires and several men had come over to the barn for the event and everyone seemed in a fine mood. Butchering a pig was always a sign that good food was on the way and that naturally put people in a good frame of mind. A butchering was also sort of a social event and everyone pitched in and helped get the job done. At the end of the day they all left the Pruitt barn with a little package of meat or bones, or something or other from the hog for their trouble. All except the balls. Mountain oysters. When Herschel butchered a boar hog he always kept the balls for himself. One of the balls he fried in its own little fat. The other he ate raw. He liked them so much he would hardly ever cut a young boar, preferring to let him grow up with his balls on. Herschel knew that boar meat was supposed to be tougher and not taste as good, but he didn't care — he wanted the balls. He never would admit it, but he liked them because he thought they made him virile. It's doubtful if anyone in Crum, other than the teachers, knew the meaning of the word virile, but they all knew fucking and Herschel believed that hog balls would keep his dick up far past his time.

Mule was waiting for me and we took our usual seats on the highest fence rail, next to the barn. The pig was enormous, one of Herschel's boars, a walking meat market. And meaner than hell. It was snuffling around in the pen, wondering why it hadn't been fed that morning, and watching the steam rise off the kettles of boiling water — boiling water made the bristles scrape off easier. Now and then the boar would charge the fence, just to watch some of the men peel off the top rail and hit the ground, almost pissing in their pants.

I'd never seen a pig being that nervous. He seemed to know that something was going to happen, something he wasn't going to like at all. There were too many men there, too much activity. He could smell the odd, acrid stench that rose from the fires under the kettles. He snorted and snuffed, he charged the fence, he dug at the ground with his snout and his feet. He tossed his head and drops of foam from his mouth sprayed into the air. And he waited, tense, fearful, angry.

I knew this pig. When Mule and I would cut across the field beside the barn, we would climb the fence of the pig sty. This pig would charge out of the mud and muck, squealing and snorting, smashing against the fence to knock us off. If we had fallen in the boar would have thrashed hell out of us in short order. I wouldn't be sorry to see this one go.

Herschel got out his kill tools. Usually, he used a .22 rifle, but he also had a hammer, knife and a huge mallet he used on special occasions, like when he was butchering a prize pig. Today Herschel decided to use the rifle and he leaned on the fence and lined up his shot. He had to wait until the boar turned in a certain direction, so he could place the shot in the side of the neck just behind the skull. That way, you saved the brain. The pig wasn't cooperating and just wouldn't get in the right position to suit Herschel — besides, Herschel was enjoying the attention he was getting. So we sort of settled down to wait.

When the rifle finally went off the pig jumped and squealed and ran around the pen. He stopped in the middle, the small hole in the side of his neck squirting blood, then ran around some more, staggering and reeling, but still refusing to go down. Herschel's shot must have been just a little bit off, a little too far away from the skull, or something. The bullet had not torn up any instantly fatal thing, and the damn pig just refused to fall over.

Herschel was embarrassed since he was widely known as the best pig killer in Crum. Being the artist that he was, Herschel wouldn't shoot again but would finish the pig off in some other way, and the sooner he did it the more face he would save in the process. It was obvious that the damn pig was not going to fall over without some more help.

Herschel decided on the hammer. He put the rifle away, picked up the hammer and turned toward the fence. The pig was getting weaker. It went down on its knees, struggled up again and made a weaving round of the pen. Its squeals were high-pitched and the blood still pumped out of the little round hole. Herschel hurried toward the fence. If the pig fell and couldn't get up again, Herschel would have to hit him where he lay. And that was bad. You should either kill the pig with the first shot or you should hit him as he stands. But you don't finish him on the ground, not if you're the best pig killer in Wayne County.

Herschel climbed to the top of the fence and started down the other side. He dropped the hammer, bent over to pick it up, still had one foot on a fence rail, lost his balance and fell. A couple of the men laughed and Herschel got red in the face. He got to his feet, picked up the hammer and advanced on the pig, the muscles in his arm standing out as he gripped the handle, his mouth set in a hard line, embarrassment and anger in his eyes. The pig, much weaker now, turned to look at Herschel — at Herschel, the man who brought the slop each morning and evening, the man who built the pen and poured the blue-john into the trough, the man who had just put a small hole in the side of his pink neck. Herschel turned sideways, to face in the same direction as the pig, so that when he swung the hammer it would be straight down into the skull between the eyes, just like driving a nail. The pig wobbled and tried to keep its head from sagging to the ground. Herschel raised his arm and brought the hammer sharply down, fury in his swing. The pig's head turned slightly at the last moment, and the hammer didn't meet its target solidly. It struck the pig's thick skull, bounced off and hit Herschel on the knee.

The pig went down instantly, its head hitting the ground at the same moment as its body. And Herschel went down too. He leaped into the air and then crashed down on top of the pig, rolling onto the stinking ground of the pig sty, screaming and clutching his knee with both hands. He flipped over on his back and sort of flopped around. Two of the men jumped into the pen and picked him up, trying not to jangle the knee. Mule, and I jumped in, too, but they just shoved us out of the way. Mule's face was tight and white — he'd never seen his father hurt in any way. I didn't know what to do, so I just stood there with a lopsided grin on my face.

They loaded Herschel in the back of a pickup truck and his wife came running from the house and tried to get a look at the wound. There was no blood. Herschel's pants leg wasn't even torn. It was just that Herschel had blown his knee apart with his own kill hammer.

One of the men got into the back of the truck with Herschel and the other got in to drive. Mule tried to go along but the men shoved him out again. They were going to take Herschel to the nearest doctor, in Kermit, and it would take them half an hour or more to get there by the time they got off the dirt roads and across the railroad tracks.

No one else made a move. No one spoke. Mule just stared after the dust of the departing truck. And then the damn pig made a faint squeal. I couldn't believe it. That sonofabitchin' pig was still alive.

Mule walked over to the fence. He stared into the pen for a moment, then picked up Herschel's kill knife and climbed inside. The pig was lying there, unable to get up but still alive. The blood was coming slowly now and the animal was unconscious. Mule bent down, grabbed an ear and pulled the head to one side, then carefully and deeply he cut the throat from ear to ear as far down as he could reach before the ground stopped the progress of the knife. He straightened up, punched the knife into the fence, and climbed over. Then, without a word, he walked away down the dirt road.

A busted leg and a pig killing, all on the same day. Folks just hadn't seen that before.

The whole thing wasn't a total loss. One of Tyler Wilson's friends came down and finished the butchering and I talked him into giving me the bladder anyway. We had a bunch of good football games with that bladder, more than with any other I can remember. It lasted a long time; it didn't rot as fast as some of the others we had played with. I don't know how many football games we might have gotten out of it if it hadn't been for Ralph Parsons. Ralph showed up one day with one of his big stray mutts, a hound that looked almost as big as the dog we sent down the river. Ralph sent the dog into the game and the sonofabitch ate the football.

WINTER

Chapter 12

Winters in Crum were a pain in the ass. It was impossible to go anywhere without getting mud up to your armpits. Half-crippled cars that still ran on the roads of summer became total losses, captives, on the muddy winter lanes. The river bank was too wet for sitting and it was too cold to hold a rifle steady when you were standing up. Not even the Kentucky pig fuckers came down to the river.

The kids would stay pretty close to home in the winter, especially the girls. For some reason, their families wouldn't let them run around the town the way they would in the summer. The rest of us, the boys, were always trying to find something to do to break up the gray and the damp and the boredom. Sometimes during the dark hours of winter evenings I would look around my room and wonder who really lived there, who really had been meant to live there, how the hell anybody *could* live there. I lived in a shed nailed to the back of a board shack on the side of a hill above a highway. The back of the wood-burning cookstove in the kitchen stuck through the wall, and that was my heat. When the December morning winds struggled against the walls of the shed, I would shiver under thin blankets and old quilts pulled up to my eyes and wait for the back of the stove to warm my forehead. Only when the stove began to glow a soft, cherry red would I ease out from beneath the covers. On the other hand, in the summer, when Mattie was cooking in the kitchen, the back of the stove would heat up and turn my shed into a baking oven. You couldn't go in there when that happened, so I would sleep outside, up on the side of the hill above the house, and hope that the damn place would burn down. I had a few treasures in my shed, like an old single-shot .22 rifle, and every now and then I would collect them all, carry them up on the hill, hide them under a rock overhang, and then go back to watch the shack, to wait for it to burst into flames. But it never did. I don't know why I didn't put the flame to it myself. I guess I felt that whoever was responsible for putting me there was damn well responsible for burning that shack, and I damn well wasn't going to do the job for them.

It wasn't that I didn't like Mattie and Oscar, and even their girls when they were in town. It's just that the shack and the tiny shed on the back of it seemed the only thing that held me in Crum. And I used to think that, if the shack went away, so could I. I never thought about the fact that that shack was a home, a home in which two nice people lived quiet, decent and loving lives. I never thought that that shack, that house, that home, was important to someone. And because I was a kid, it never occurred to me to be grateful for what I did have. It was not important to me, and that's all I knew at the time.

The stove did have some uses. I took an old coffee can, a big one, and attached it with some baling wire, the bottom of the can resting flush against the stove. I put some rocks in the can and used the can's metal top to seal everything inside. When the rocks got hot the can made a sort of oven, and I could put a potato in there to bake. One morning I put some eggs in a tiny can of water and put them in my coffee can to boil. I was going to take them to school, only I forgot. Sometime during the day the water boiled away and the eggs began to burn. Egg smoke came out of the can and into the shed, and then seeped into the house. I don't think I had ever smelled real egg smoke before that day, and I really hope I don't ever smell it again. I would rather stomp on another burning bag of shit. Mattie had been working down at Luke's and she wasn't there when the damned eggs began to burn. But when she got home it didn't take her long to find out what was going on, to discover my coffee can oven. She cleaned up the egg mess and aired out my shed before I got home. I guess she had to do that, just so the smell wouldn't keep seeping into the house. It was nice of her. Of course, she also nailed my shed door shut, and then hid the hammer. It was full dark before I got the nails out and got back into the shed.

Sometimes, in the early winter morning, before school, when the stove glowed with the heat that helped me out of bed, I would take a potato I had baked the night before, warm it up in the coffee can oven, and then climb to the top of the hill behind the shack and watch the world get brighter. I would eat the hot potato and sit on the hill and blow puffs of frosty breath and look at the rows of ridges running away from me, up and down the valley. Down below I could see the river, looking clean and beautiful, and I could look directly across it to the first row of hills in Kentucky. The hill I sat on was the highest in the area and if you didn't go too far into the trees the view was good. Not great, because you had a view of Crum. But good, because you could see the other hills.

And that was what we had around Crum — hills. The hills, in ridges and folds and ranks, stood away from the river in waves of green and black in the summer, brown and gray in the winter. The river wore its way down among them and the little side streams that came into the river carved the hollers where people built houses. The hollers were steep and narrow, and only when a small, flat space was left by the carving streams could you put a house flat on the ground, just the way you'd want it. And then, of course, a really heavy rain would come every ten years or so and cause water to build up in the hollers and come crashing down through the narrow drainages, a fast-rising irresistible force of brown foam and debris. And it would take out all the houses. When the water was gone the people would build their houses back again. It was their land, and that's where they would put their houses, floods or no floods. That was just part of living in the hollers.

All the ridges and hills were forested and they all seemed almost the same height, and when you stood on one you could only see to the next one where there'd be more trees and thickets. What lay beyond was again a mystery until you climbed down into a holler, then up the next ridge to the top, only to see another, almost identical, ridge in the near distance.

The name of the hill I was on was really Beecher's Mountain, but it was the one we always called Shit Hill. One of our favorite things to do was to sneak away from school, cross the tracks and the highway and climb the hill to a clearing that was near the top and which overlooked the school. There, in full view of the noontime crowd on the football field, we would drop our pants and empty our bowels. Of course, you couldn't really see us from the school unless you knew exactly where to look, but that didn't matter. We made our point, and it made winter a little more interesting.

Chapter 13

Miss Thatcher was short, plump, plain, clean and smelled good. She also had the most delicious tits we had ever seen, which she strapped tightly to her chest underneath long-sleeved, high-necked blouses that didn't show a thing. But there was no way you could completely hide a pair like hers, and Miss Thatcher knew we liked to stare at them. They led the way down the hallway whenever she left the classroom, and they were the first things to enter the room when she returned. They were magnificent. They pressed against her blouse, straining to burst free into the room. We spent whole days admiring them. When we stared too hard, Miss Thatcher would get so uncomfortable that she would leave — that was unheard-of delicacy for Crum.

I liked Miss Thatcher a lot, but my liking was nothing compared to the way Benny liked her. Benny liked tits, all tits, but he liked Miss Thatcher's most of all because he thought they liked him. He wanted to let Miss Thatcher know that he wanted them and he figured it was just a matter of time before he was rolling them around in his hands and taking little naps all snuggled up between them.

The problem with Benny was that when he liked a girl, he announced the fact by whipping out his dick and pointing it at her. That was probably the way Miss Thatcher was going to be informed and we eagerly waited for Benny to declare his love. Miss Thatcher's subject was English and Benny wasn't exactly entranced by it. He was in the class only because the school told him he had to be. Actually, Benny could hardly read, which is one reason he spent most class time with his dick in his hand.

It was a winter afternoon and just after noon and the sky was so dark that it looked like evening. It was one of those

God-awful winter days when the sky just doesn't press down against the mountaintops, it presses down against your chest. There was a permanent dampness about the winters in Crum — the air was wet, but it wasn't raining. The worst thing was that there was no color. Everything was gray. Flat. The sky seemed to pick up off the floor of the valley and rise in a gray sheet, hiding the tops of the hills. Cars would enter Crum out of the ghostly gray, and they would leave the same way. For all I knew it could have been the same car, just coming and going, gray, gray, gray. I used to pray for rain or snow, just to have a change.

The lights were on in the gray damp classroom and Miss Thatcher was teaching us about something. I don't remember what, but she was teaching us something and working hard. And Benny decided it was time to do it. I don't know why he waited so many months. He must have really loved her. He got his dick out, just sort of waving it lazily back and forth in his hand. Miss Thatcher was up at the front of the room and Benny was trying to decide how to get her back where he was sitting without letting her know what he had for her. Miss Thatcher was very involved in whatever she was teaching us, and she swept back and forth across the front of the room, her favorite textbook in her hand, her voice rising and falling as she floated on the lines. She lost track of us completely and was in a world of another time, another place, a world where men were gentlemen and didn't stare for hours at a lady's tits. She went on for a full ten minutes, now and then brushing a stray lock of her light brown hair back away from her forehead.

Suddenly she stopped. There wasn't a sound in the classroom. She realized that she had gotten carried away and that she was breathing in sharp, short rushes. She had sweated dark moisture stains under her arms and around her stomach. She closed her book and carefully laid it on her desk, turned and walked slowly down the aisle toward the back of the classroom. As she walked, she commented on the lines she had been citing, trying to bring some sense of order to her own thinking. As she passed each row the kids turned their heads to follow her progress to the back of the room, knowing what she was getting closer and closer to. When Benny decided to go into his act, it was the only time the whole year the room was totally silent.

But it was odd. Nip was in the class, sitting a couple of desks away from Benny. He was the only kid in class who did not have his eyes locked to Miss Thatcher. He just sat there, staring down at his desk.

Then she was there. At the back of the room. At Benny's desk. Benny sat quietly, dick in hand, looking lovingly up at Miss Thatcher, who kept on talking softly. As she talked, her eyes slowly riveted on what Benny was cradling with his left hand, holding out from beneath the arm of his school desk. He wanted Miss Thatcher to get a good look at it. Maybe he hoped she'd be so impressed, she'd fall in love right there.

"So you see, Benny," Miss Thatcher said, "the essence of good writing is not just in the words as they are written, but in the deeper meanings they have for the people who read them . . ."

Her voice gradually trailed away. We braced ourselves for what we thought would come next. I expected a faint, I knew Mule had his money on a scream and Elvira said that Miss Thatcher would probably wet her pants. Ruby wouldn't talk about it. She knew that I liked Miss Thatcher, and anything that kept me out from under Ruby's thumb, even if I was just thinking about it, Ruby didn't like.

We waited. Miss Thatcher just stared down at Benny. There had been nothing in Miss Thatcher's training for this moment, nothing in the teacher's manual. So she stared, saying nothing, and large tears began to form in the wells of her eyes. They brimmed, burst and flowed silently down her cheeks and all the while she said nothing, just standing there waiting for the world to correct itself.

Slowly and delicately Miss Thatcher turned toward the door, her footsteps hardly making a sound as her small feet took her away. She opened the door, turned, looked at the class for a moment, the tears still streaming down and dripping onto the tops of her wonderful breasts. She went through the door and was gone.

The class period was only about half over and so we sat there, waiting for Miss Thatcher to return. No one said anything. We stared out the window, the girls opened a few books and Benny put his thing away. Miss Thatcher hadn't liked what he had done, she had cried, and Benny was disturbed. He didn't understand when people did nothing when he flashed. It just wasn't natural. Gradually, we began to talk back and forth and the class period wore on. Pretty soon it was too late to go out after Miss Thatcher anyway. The bell rang and we left the room.

Miss Thatcher did not come to any of her other classes that day. We sort of expected that. We knew she might even try to get Benny kicked out of school. When you think about it, it's a wonder he had been allowed to stay as long as he had.

The next day we wandered into our classes, waiting for someone to come and get Benny and toss him out. But no one came. And Miss Thatcher didn't come to school, either. Benny was very quiet and, for a change, he didn't play with himself for the entire day. Elvira said that Miss Thatcher didn't come because the size of what she had seen had scared her. Ethan Piney tried to convince Benny that he should go and see Miss Thatcher and show her his tool again, just so she would know that it wouldn't hurt her. For a minute or two, we thought Benny might actually do that.

It turned out that none of the teachers or even the principal had seen Miss Thatcher. When she didn't show up yet another day, the principal asked Coach Mason to go and talk to her. If anybody had the touch to talk Miss Thatcher back into the classroom, it would be Coach Mason. There was a small house behind Tyler Wilson's store, owned by a widow who rented out a spare bedroom to teachers. That's where Miss Thatcher was staying. But when the Coach got to the house, the landlady said Miss Thatcher had left, had come home early from school two day's before and just packed up and left. The landlady didn't know why. Miss Thatcher had said nothing.

And so she was gone. We never knew to where, or how, but she was gone. She was gone from Crum and from high school boys who take out their dicks in the classroom, gone from people who did not appreciate other people who could write things and yet others who could read them with feeling. She was gone from the damp and the cold and the gray mud. She was gone from outside toilets that sent their stink for two hundred yards in all directions. The delicacy of the Miss

Thatchers of the world could not stomach what we were and so they closed the door and left us.

The substitute English teacher was a man. He started out the first class by declaring that the Bible was the only book really worth reading, and that we would read a part of it, aloud and together, each and every day.

❄

Chapter 14

Miss Thatcher was gone, we read our Bible every day in class, we learned that no man is without sin, his days are short, and the whole thing was pain in the ass.

It was either cold, or wet, or cold *and* wet and the winter slapped Crum into the ground and brought what life there was to a standstill. Now and then what we called a storm would bang into the valley and the wind would slam down a couple of trees somewhere on the hillsides. But we were too protected by the hills to lose anything more than a tree or two, except for the gust that took the huge wooden sign off the front of Tyler Wilson's General Store. The sign sailed off like a misshapen kite, spinning and bouncing along the road and leaping smack into the middle of Homer Wiley's chicken coop.

The classes at school dragged with a monotony that made thoughts of spring ring and glow in my mind until my ears could hear the imaginary rustle of tree leaves. I longed for something, anything, to break the endless string of days, dark days, cold days, wet days, and gray days that had no reason to be.

The day Constable Clyde Prince's outhouse exploded was the answer to my prayers, or so I thought. The old outhouse flew to pieces about three o'clock on a frigid Saturday afternoon and by four o'clock Clyde was on the lookout for Mule and me. And Clyde could chase. He had a gun and he was the constable and he was built like a buggy whip bent double. He was tall and rangy and his brown eyes were so dark that you couldn't see into them. Clyde was lean and hard and he was damned good looking. I guess that's the way he got his beautiful wife, Genna. He sure as hell didn't have much else going for him.

There was something going on here that Mule and I couldn'tfigure out — Clyde got onto us too quickly; he came looking for us too fast. He must have had help. I bet Ethan, that sonofabitch, turned us in.

Actually, he was wrong. It was Wade who bombed the out-house, and he did a really wonderful job of it. When Wade was little he lived with some people who worked in the mines and Wade knew all about dynamite and stuff like that. Wade rigged a charge and lowered it by the wires right down through one of the holes — Clyde's outhouse was a two-holer — and then backed off to the end of the wires and touched it off with a car battery. The depth of the hole had kept the contents from freezing, and when the dynamite went off the whole stinking mess made a sticky, dark cloud that dappled the countryside — including Clyde's house — with splotches of brown, bits of wood, and soggy, colored scraps of old catalog pages. Every single splotch froze solid upon contact. As I said, it was a beautiful job. Wade was a real artist.

Mule and I had been down at the river shooting at floating cans and bottles and bits of ice. We were huddled against the bank, trying to keep from shaking long enough to aim when Nip found us. He had been in Tyler Wilson's store when Clyde came in and as soon as he left, Nip came straight to the river bank.

We really didn't want Clyde to find us. He was a simple, mean sonofabitch who liked to wear his gun and his little badge and give people a hard time. Clyde didn't fuck around with the men in Crum too much, though. He had to live there and the men didn't take too kindly to being messed with. But we didn't count. So we sat there in the gray cold and held a war council. There wasn't much chance of calling the whole thing an acci-dent. I mean, shithouses just didn't explode by themselves and, like I said, we didn't know who had done it. We figured that by the time we found out who it was, Clyde would have us locked up in the jail upriver in Kermit, and it wouldn't do us any good to worry about it then. We'd probably never get out. At least not until Clyde thought we were too old to bother with wanting to get into Genna's pants. And that would take about fifty years.

Mule was for staying on the river bank. Clyde would never find us there, not if we didn't want him to, and even if he did we had the rifle and we could just shoot the bastard. But it was too cold for that, and besides I wanted to see what Clyde's house looked like with all those frozen clumps of shit all over it. Come spring, it would be a good bet that Clyde wouldn't be able to stay at home for very long on warm afternoons.

Nip was undecided. He didn't want to leave us and miss any of the excitement, but he didn't want to stay with us, either. Finally, his curiosity got the better of him and he said that if we were going to see Clyde's house he would come with us. So we left the river. As soon as we started finding frozen pieces of shit, we stopped. We were close enough to see the dappling on the house and to notice that where the outhouse had stood that there was now a hole about half again bigger than the one Clyde originally had dug there. The outhouse itself was absolutely gone. The largest piece left was a four-foot length of two-by-four, sticking down through the roof of Clyde's house. It was a perfect job.

Actually, I wasn't sorry to see Clyde's outhouse gone, or any outhouse for that matter. I hated shithouses. I would never go into one of the huge outhouses out behind the school. They were full to the bursting point anyway, and the kids who couldn't wait just pissed against a wall or through a crack to the outside, and the place was so rank that it took your breath away. I have to admit, though, there really were some interesting outhouses in Crum if you cared enough to look. On the way to Kermit there was one place where a small stream went under the road through a huge concrete culvert. Up the stream about fifty yards and visible from the highway there was an outhouse built out over the water. There was no hole in the ground, of course, just the moving stream underneath flowing straight to the good people of Crum, Kenova, Ashland and Cincinnati. And I remember another one with a pair of old wagon wheels bolted to the side. When the hole filled up, they just dug another hole, tipped the outhouse over onto its wheels, and rolled it to the new hole.

When we had admired the damage for about ten minutes, Clyde's wife, Genna, came out of the house and walked toward the hole in the ground. As she neared the hole her pace slowed and she gazed up and into the woods. She had on a short wool jacket and jeans and was wearing a pair of women's work shoes. She was clearly the sexiest married woman in Crum.

Genna stood there, looking first up into the woods and then at the hole in the ground and it suddenly dawned on me that she had to go to the toilet. She turned and started walking up the hill toward the woods.

When we realized where she was going, the three of us backed away from our hiding place and, crouching low, ran in a wide circle around and up the hill, trying to beat her to the trees. We sure as hell weren't going to miss a chance to see Genna drop her pants. Genna walked slowly up the hill, pausing now and then to look behind her at the house below and the highway beyond, then turning to inspect the trees, trying to pick a spot where she couldn't be seen from the road. Mule whispered that he and Nip were going on up the hill, to a spot where they could get a better view. They backed away from the thicket, moving silently through the woods.

I couldn't take my eyes off Genna. She eased up the hill, a step at a time, and then turned and angled straight for my thicket. I knew Mule and Nip had gone too far. They couldn't see her. I also knew that if she wanted to use my thicket she would see me and that that would ruin the whole thing. But she was too close now for me to do anything except stay put. I was trapped.

She came around the top of the thicket and turned to face the road, and looked me full in the face. Her expression said nothing. She made no sound, nothing. Her look was blank. My face glowed in the late afternoon cold and I tried desperately to think of something to say, anything to remotely explain my being there.

And so I said, in a choking voice, "Anything I can do to help?"

She took a step towards me, almost within arm's reach, and then lifted the front of her jacket. With her other hand she unbuttoned her jeans and pushed them down to her knees. She wasn't wearing any panties. Clyde didn't deserve this, was all I could think. It was just too great for him. Her thighs were perfect and tapered, sculpted and solid, and slightly open as she stood there with her legs spread tight against her dropped jeans. She raised her hands to the jacket again and unbuttoned it. It was one of those jackets that have a cotton blanket for a lining and as she opened it I could see red and black stripes. The jacket fell open and there was nothing underneath except Genna. She was naked under the jacket and the jeans and I thought I would faint just from the sight of her.

I imagine I actually felt the warmth radiating from her body, and while I was reeling from the nearness of her, Genna slowly squatted in front of me and urinated. The pattering of the water on the dead leaves carried my attention to the ground beneath her, to the steam rising as the warm liquid ran down the hill. I thought of Benny and Elvira on the river bank. Jesus, it was almost too much and it was happening again, only this time it was Elvira's *mother*, for chrissake — well, not really her mother, but close enough — and this time it was happening to me. I reached my hand toward her.

She didn't even seem to notice, just took a piece of paper from her coat pocket and carefully blotted herself. She stood up, again exposing the full length of her body to me. Her jacket had slipped closed and she slowly opened it, arching her back and stretching as she raised her hands to the jacket. Her stretching and the arch of her back forced her hips in my direction, almost as if she were offering them to me. She reached down and pulled her jeans slowly up her legs. She buttoned her pants, tugged her coat closed and took three steps and was past me. Then she stopped.

She turned and stepped up to me and her jacket fell open and those perfect breasts were there within my reach and I could smell the warmth of her. And even when I knew that she was drawing back her fist it really didn't register until I felt the sharp bones of her hand drive into my belly just above my belt buckle, felt my stomach being shoved out of the way as her arm reached for my backbone. My bowels went loose and I clamped down on them in a wave of nausea. I folded over and fell back on my ass and she stood over me, her slight frame drawn tight and angry. Her words barely came through the roaring in my ears.

"You want to lay the meat to me? Who the hell do you think you are, you fucking hillbilly! Only men fuck me! You want to lay me, you got to come through the front door and

ask for it like a man, not hide behind the bushes like a dog!"
And she turned and went down the hill.

Mule and I slept in his dad's barn that night, buried deep
within the loose hay. I got there before Mule and wrapped up
in my favorite horse blanket and burrowed into my favorite
place, knowing that Mule would find me. It was warm down
there and gradually my stomach began to unwind. All I thought
about was Genna and how she said you had to come through
the door like a man.

When Mule showed up I told him that I had a stomach
ache from something I ate. And I told him that Genna had
gone out of sight of me, too, and that I didn't get to see her
drop her pants. Anyway, he wouldn't have believed me if I had
told the truth.

The next morning we talked it over and decided to just
give ourselves up and try to convince the Constable that we
didn't blow up his shithouse. We weren't going to walk right
up to him, though, because there was no telling what he would
do. Since it was Sunday, we decided to go by the church and
give ourselves up to Parson Piney. Right after Halloween the
good parson had preached against us for four straight weeks,
and he wouldn't have stopped then except that his flock was
getting a bit restless hearing about boys who had hit his wife
with a rotten apple. Parson Piney had gotten us out of his system, we thought, and we also figured that if we turned ourselves in right after the Sunday morning services, in broad daylight, the parson wasn't likely to kick hell out of us in front of
his entire congregation.

We stood outside the church waiting for the end of the
services. We heard the old piano bang out the last notes of a
hymn, giving the sinners one final chance to come forward and
be saved. Parson Piney would be the first to the door, since he
always came out as the concluding hymn was playing. We were
less and less sure we had made the right decision when the
door burst open and there stood the parson, looking ready to
take on the devil in hand-to-hand combat.

He saw us instantly.

"Sinners!" the parson screamed. "Despoilers of houses of
relief!"

Mule and I took a step backwards. The parson knew about the outhouse and thought we had done it. I could feel Mule fading away at my side and edging backwards, towards the railroad track.

But it was too late. Faces appeared behind the parson and people began to ease out of the church, glancing at the righteous bulk of the parson and then at us, waiting for the wrath of God to strike us, to slam us into the earth for the enormity of our sins, to punish us for all the evil and vile acts of our lives, and especially for blowing up the shithouse. The parson thundered down the church stairs.

Mule broke for the railroad tracks. The parson never hesitated. He came straight ahead, drawing back his mighty ham of a fist as he came, and hit me full in the face. Suddenly I was floating in the air, just lying right out in the air, horizontal, and then I hit the ground, nose first into the gravel in front of the church. The ground seemed sticky and I knew that blood was pouring from my face and mixing with dirt and gravel. Dimly, I could hear running feet and I knew they had caught up to Mule.

Fifteen minutes later we were in Tyler Wilson's store. Tyler had been in church and volunteered to open his store so they could take us there for questioning. The parson and several other good people of the church came, and someone went off to get Clyde. Herschel Pruitt hobbled in on a cane. I wondered if he remembered that I had sort of laughed at him when he broke his knee with his own pig-killing hammer. Anyway, it was lucky for Mule that his father was there.

I tried to look and act calm, but I was really scared. I had been in that store hundreds of times, but I had never thought of it as a jail before. It was just one large room, longer than it was wide, shelves on each side and a high ceiling. On the left there was a counter that ran from the front of the store all the way to the rear, a counter that had glass-paneled cases where Tyler kept those things that he wanted you to see but not touch. In the middle of the counter there was a space large enough to walk through, and behind that space there was a door that led to Tyler's office. The door to that office was always closed.

There weren't any women in the store. I wished there

had been. I couldn't remember anybody in West Virginia having been lynched for blowing up an outhouse, but there was always a first time and I thought that if there was a woman or two in the crowd that the thing might go a bit more calmly. Then I thought that Clyde might bring Genna with him, and that got me thinking on another track — I would confess to blowing up the outhouse just to get it over with, just to get out of the room, to get away from Genna. I was afraid to have her look at me.

My face was a mask of blood and dirt. Mule kept staring at me and I realized that he wasn't the only one. Everyone was looking at me. It was plainer than hell that whoever had fingered me for the outhouse job had fingered me alone. Mule had just been brought along for the ride.

Clyde came in and he was alone. I didn't think Clyde would do anything to us in front of all those witnesses, and we might be able to convince him that we were telling the truth. Then I remembered that we *would* be telling the truth, that we really *hadn't* blown up the outhouse, that we were — that I was — *innocent*! I was so used to be being to blame that it took a while for me to remember that I really *was* innocent. Goddamn!

Clyde conferred briefly with the parson, but before they could get some sort of plan going I started talking. The truth was too simple and too easy and so I took off on the goddamndest lie that I had ever heard. The more I talked, the more interested I became in how it would end because I had no idea. And now I couldn't tell it again if my life depended on it. All I remember is that somewhere in all the garbage that came out I told the assembled good people that I couldn't possibly have done it, that, by God, I was innocent.

Tyler sat in his big chair behind the counter, smoking a cigar and enjoying the inquisition. When I paused in my story long enough to catch my breath, he took out his stogie and inspected the end of it.

"Son," he said, "I don't think you've explained the situation the way we want to hear it. Maybe we need to do some more explaining to you."

Clyde cussed and fumed and stomped up and down. The

parson mumbled a prayer, not praying for anybody in particular, but making enough noise to let everyone know he was still there and interested. Everybody else dipped fingers into barrels of this and that, nibbling at things they wouldn't have had the nerve to sample if the store had been open for business.

Tyler made no move to break up the gathering, so things got worse. I repeated to Clyde that I didn't know who had done it, but that it wasn't me. It was just that simple. Clyde decided that it *was* me, no matter what I said, for one equally simple reason — he *wanted* it to be me. There was a lot of shouting back and forth and Clyde got madder and madder and Tyler sat up on the edge of his chair. And that's when Clyde grabbed me. I wasn't handcuffed or anything — I don't think Clyde owned any. I was just sitting there in a straight-back chair and then Clyde grabbed me and threw me across the room at the door to Tyler's little office. I slammed into the door and Clyde was on me, pushing me hard against the wood. He turned the knob and I exploded into the office. The door slammed behind me just as the first punch caught me in the side. I felt a rib give way. Clyde spun me around and drilled me into the wall, ramming his hand under my chin to force my head back. He brought up his other fist and opened his fingers and I thought he was going to slap me. Instead, he ground the heel of his hand into my injured nose.

"You want to fuck my wife? Let's see if she likes your looks when you walk around with this nose, you smart sonofabitch!" And he ground his hand into my face again.

Desperate, I brought a knee up into his groin. Clyde gagged and snapped over, letting go of me and holding his balls with both hands. He fell back against the wall so hard that a picture hanging there crashed to the floor, sending little shards flying.

I should have made a break for the door while I had the chance, but I couldn't see clearly. I took a few seconds to straighten myself out, and that was a mistake. Clyde recovered. He was up off the floor and on me again, this time bouncing his fist off the left side of my head like he was beating a drum.

I heard Tyler Wilson's voice through the pain. He was yelling at somebody and then the door to the office broke open and Aaron Mason was there. I had never realized how strong the Coach really was. Oh, he had bounced us around on the football field now and then, when he was feeling particularly playful, but that was different. Now, here, the damn door almost blew off the hinges. He just hit it with his shoulder and it came apart. He lunged into the room and grabbed Clyde by the head and slammed him to the floor. Before Clyde could make a move, he brought Clyde's arm up behind him and, grabbing a handful of Clyde's ass, lifted his whole body off the floor. The coach threw Clyde through the door, over the counter, and back out into the store. Clyde landed with his face jammed against a flour barrel.

I was carried back to the straight-backed chair. The room was still. The men didn't know what to do now, and they didn't know what Aaron would do, either. The pot-bellied stove in the center of the floor was cold and outside the gray of winter afternoon clamped its absolute stillness over Crum. The Coach stood silently, looking into everyone's face. They had let Clyde do whatever he had it mind to do and just stood around enjoying the show. Aaron Mason didn't have to say a word. They could see what he thought of them.

Clyde rolled over behind him and tried to pull out his gun. The beating had left him groggy and he didn't do a very good job of it. The gun wasn't in a holster, just jammed down into his front pants pocket, and the hammer got caught as he tried to pull it out. Just as the gun came free Aaron clamped his hand over the whole pistol, his fingers covering the cylinder and squeezing until his knuckles went white. If Clyde pulled the trigger, there's no way that cylinder would have turned. I had never seen anybody do that before — grab a gun like that and just refuse to let it fire. The Coach twisted his hand slowly and the gun oozed out of Clyde's grip. Clyde started to whimper something about the law, and Aaron brought his other arm around and whipped it across Clyde's mouth. You could have heard the crack all the way down at the school. Clyde's mouth turned into a red mess, and the noises stopped coming out.

Aaron popped open the cylinder with one hand, shook all the bullets out, then threw the weapon toward the rear of the store with all his might. It hit something back there that was glass and that broke. Tyler Wilson didn't say a thing.

We all stood there in the gloom of a general store on Sunday, looking at each other, not knowing what was coming next. There was a roaring in my ears. Other than that, only the sounds of breathing and sloppy tobacco chewing crept among the boxes and the barrels and the cans.

And in the middle of the silence there was a muffled "whooomp," a sound deep from within the earth, a low, booming resonance that rolled up the river and washed back and forth among the hollers and hills until it died away in the vastness of the mountains. And inside the store even the sounds of breathing stopped as every head was raised in sharp attention, every ear cocked toward the door. From outside the store a high, quavering voice shouted from the distance.

"Mr. Wilson! Mr. Wilson! Mr. Wilson!"

The voice got closer and gradually Tyler understood that the voice was shouting his name. Tyler stepped to the middle of the room, cupping his hand in the air at the side of his head in an effort to gather in the sound. He didn't put his hand against his ear, just held it as though to make the sound bounce off his palm. The front door of the store burst open and Nip was there, his eyes wide and excited, his breathing sharp, loud, punching the absolute silence.

"Mr. Wilson! Mr. Wilson!" he shouted, "someone just blowed up yer outhouse!"

Chapter 15

T he icy heart of the Appalachian winter seemed to beat on forever. The freezing, bone-crushing mists that passed for winter rains hung over Crum and for days on end the sun would not shine, unable to cut through the layer of insulation that hung above the valley and prevented spring from moving through the hills. The browns stayed brown and the mud stayed mud, except when it was ice, and the cold never let you forget that you were only minutes from the edge of wilderness.

In the middle of a Crum winter, I felt sure there was no escape from Crum. The chill of the days and the damp winds of the nights seemed to close off all routes out of town. The busses that went through had their windows steamed up on the inside and the passengers had no interest in wiping off the condensation. When the passenger trains shot past the school building on late winter days the lights would be on in the cars, but the people never looked out at our ramshackle houses and muddy roads. They just wanted to get out of here, get on with their train ride, get to wherever they were going and sit in front of the stove and warm their feet again on their own hearth. Sometimes I thought I could see their faces, but I never really could.

Now and then through the windows of the school, I could see people walk down the railroad track, probably on the way to the general store or the post office. They would huddle inside their coats, pulling their heads down against the damp and chill, leaning into the winds that often tore down the valley. By the time we got out of school each day the weak light had already begun to fail. The kids who rode the buses would arrive at their houses back in the hollows and on the edges of the rivers long after dark, their evening chores still in front of them. I had no chores so I would go back to my sleeping shed on the back of the house on the hill and lie on my bed, listening to the sounds coming from the kitchen. I would dream and sometimes I would scheme ways to get out of Crum.

Sometimes I'd think of Ruby, which usually took a while, and then I would inspect my possessions, the things in the world that belonged to me, the collection of junk that I wouldn't trade for anything in the world, unless it was more junk. My most valued possession was my old, single-shot rifle. Sometimes I would let the other guys shoot it, but I could shoot it better than anybody and I often had fantasies of taking the rifle and moving into the woods for good, hiding out and living off the land. On our way out of Tyler's store Mule and I had pocketed two boxes of shells — that would keep us for a while and I could some down out of the hills and take more when I needed them.

I had some other possessions, among them a one-pound coffee can on which the metal lid fit very tightly and which I kept tied under my bed, suspended from the creaking springs by a piece of string. What made the coffee can important was that it had my money in it, once as much as thirty-seven dollars. The outside of the can was absolutely shiny from being handled so much and I had lined the inside with pieces of rubber from an old inner tube so that it wouldn't rattle if it accidentally got shaken while hanging under the bed. I wrapped the money in an old T-shirt and stuffed the whole mess inside the can. It made a tight little package and I thought no one would think there was money in a can that didn't rattle.

Crum was a complete mess by early March. Mud oozed up in huge ridges on the dirt road by the railroad track, and any car or truck that ventured off the highway was sure to be in trouble. I would stay alone in my shed until I couldn't stand being cooped up any more, and then I would do anything to break the pattern. Go shooting down at the river. Climb the hill and look for likely hiding places that I might have to use sometime. And, very often, I would end up with Ruby.

I liked to go to Ruby's house. Usually, those were good times with us just lying on the floor of the parlor, talking, listening to the radio, eating popcorn. It was great to be with Ruby then. There usually were no other kids around and she didn't have to show everyone that she was in command. So it was great. Ruby was relaxed and beautiful and every now and then she would let me kiss her or do some little thing that made me feel that she wanted me there.

But on this particular Sunday afternoon she was a real bitch. She didn't want me to leave but she made me miserable the whole time. I didn't know what was going on but I knew there was no use in hanging around any longer so I left. Not before she called me a fucking dumb hillbilly bastard. I marched off the porch and into the mud and headed for the railroad tracks, the water soaking my denim jacket and running down the back of my neck. I cursed under my breath as I walked, a slow, steady, mumbled litany streaming from my mouth into the mud.

I sensed her before I actually saw her. When I shut my mouth and looked up, Yvonne was standing there by the railroad tracks. She was coming back from the store trying to keep a big brown paper sack dry between her arms. The rain had blown in under her hat and the drops clung to her face and made it glisten in the cold light. She stood there, the water running down her legs and into her shoes, and she was beautiful. Most of all, she wasn't saying a word, not a word. She wasn't calling me a hillbilly and maybe she didn't think I was stupid.

I took the paper bag from her arms, turned and started walking toward her house. She hesitated a second, then came after me. I glanced over my shoulder at Ruby's house, and I hoped I saw a curtain move in one of the front windows, but it was hard to tell through the rain.

When we got to the house I took her arm and turned her toward me.

"Can I come over and see you this evening?" I tried to say it simply and honestly, but that's not how it came out.

"Why?"

Why? Why? What the hell's going on here, I thought. I ask a girl if I can come see her and she wants to know why! I looked hard to get some sort of signal.

"Look," she said, "I'm glad you walked home with me, but why don't you go back to Ruby's later on . . . I don't want . . . maybe you'd be better off over there."

"No!" I said sharply. She had me pegged, all right. She didn't want to be used as a stand-in for anybody.

"I just want to be here for a while, Yvonne. Just here. Can I come?"

"If you don't talk about Ruby," she said. "You can come over if you don't talk about her. I don't want to listen to anything like that."

She left me there outside the door, feeling warmer by the minute, wondering if maybe I hadn't made a mistake, wondering about my choice of women, wondering if I had any brains at all. I went straight back to my shed and got out my coffee can. I took out a crumpled five-dollar bill and tucked it carefully into the watch pocket of my jeans.

When I got to Yvonne's that night, we had the place to ourselves. Even in the rain, her folks had gone to a revival meeting in Kermit and wouldn't be back until the preacher ran out of things to scream at the sinners. And if the preacher really knew his business and his sinners, that would take all night. Their house was built along the side of the hill, with a porch that ran all along the front. On nice days you could sit on the porch and put your feet up on the wide, low railing and look out over most of the town. And you could see the church of the Reverend Herman Piney, that sonofabitch, across the highway and the tracks and off by the side of a small corn field.

Yvonne was wearing a white blouse and a full, blue skirt, but she didn't have any shoes on. Somehow, her bare feet made her look like she really belonged there, like she had been waiting all day for me to come home. It was one wonderful feeling. The living room was heated with a small, open gas stove that sat in a fake fireplace in the corner. She had the heater turned up high, the flames making the ceramic grate glow. We turned off the lights and sat in the glow of the heater, trying to listen to the radio. There was too much static because of the weather and just when we finally gave up tuning the thing the electricity went off and the radio died. We talked and we talked and pretty soon we even laughed a little and both of us began to relax and discover that we really liked to be there together with only the glow of the heater radiating out from the far corner of the room.

I was careful not to say anything about Ruby, or about anything that Ruby was even connected with, and Yvonne didn't bring up the subject either. At first it was difficult to remember to keep my mouth shut about things like that, but after a while it got easy, very easy.

Later Yvonne went into the kitchen and got a bottle of beer and a couple of glasses. We split the beer and sat on the sofa, sipping at the glasses and leaning toward each other until suddenly the glasses were on the floor and Yvonne and I were wrapped around each other, crushing each other back against the sofa, working mouth against mouth. Our mouths stayed together through the droning of the winter rain, through the tangle of arms and legs, through the rolling and turning. We were deep within the pillows of the sofa, twisting and reaching, groping, making low sounds.

Sweat poured from my forehead and her face glistened as we pressed together. She forced her hands between us and unbuttoned my shirt, peeling it from me. I felt her warm breasts against my chest and in another instant she was naked. I pulled back and sat up on the edge of the sofa and explored with my eyes. I couldn't help myself. I pulled off the rest of my clothes and lay beside her, running my hands over her, wanting to know her in the smallest detail. She moved under my hands, only slightly, helping the hands along, helping them explore. She looked steadily into my eyes, with nothing to hide, and then she rolled me on top of her.

When it was finished we lay pressed together for a few minutes, neither of us wanting to make the first move to get up. Then she sat up and so did I, the two of us sitting on the sofa, naked, as though we had done this many times and it was the most natural thing in the world for us to be sitting there like that. I picked up my pants, but she put her hand on my arm and held it there until I put the pants down again. The small room was warm from our bodies and from the gas heater and our sweat stayed on our skins and shone in the dim reflection of the flames. The rain had stopped and the silence that comes after a rain was on the house and the dark town. Through the window I could see that the heavy clouds were moving down the valley and that, somewhere up there, a bright moon was struggling its way through.

She kissed me, then got up and walked toward the kitchen, her step like a dancer's, holding her shining body perfectly erect. I followed her into the kitchen. She went to a shelf and got a couple of glasses and then opened the back door and took a large pitcher from the cupboard that stood outside on the back porch. The pitcher was full of buttermilk and she poured it into the glasses. We sipped the buttermilk and walked back into the living room to a window that looked out on the front porch. Down the distance we could see the tiny town lying there in darkness, with only a kerosene lamp or two flickering. A shaft of moonlight broke through the clouds now and then, dropping directly onto the valley floor.

I stood beside her, holding her hand. She stepped in front of me and pressed herself backward, firmly. He hips rubbed against me and then she stepped away and disappeared down a short hallway. In a moment she was back, wearing a bathrobe that was so big it trailed the ground behind her. It was one of those bathrobes that was made out of terry cloth like a big soft towel. She took my hand and led me to the front door. We stepped out on the cold porch and she pulled me to her, wrapping me in the bathrobe. We stood there, swaying slightly, tiny cold drops of rain brushing us, and I could feel myself hard against her stomach. She moved her feet and we shuffled over to the railing. We shivered slightly from the cold, but it wasn't nearly as bad as I thought it would be. I was almost too warm.

Yvonne scooted herself up on the flat board that ran the length of the railing. And she opened the bathrobe and wrapped me inside of it, opening her legs as I moved forward and then wrapping the bathrobe around both of us. And then she pulled me inside her.

I still had a glass of buttermilk in my hand. I fumbled around, trying to put it down, but she took it from me. She held it over her left breast, leaned forward, and tilted the glass onto her, coating her breasts with buttermilk. She locked her legs around me leaned backward, her head and shoulders suspended above Crum, above the valley, her white, dripping breasts pointed straight at the dark sky. She held the glass over her and gently tilted it, dripping buttermilk on her stomach.

As she raised herself the buttermilk ran from her breast and stomach down between her legs and onto me.

Jesus, where did she learn stuff like that? There sure wasn't anything like that described in any book I'd ever read. Yvonne sat up and pressed herself against me. The buttermilk made us slide across each other and we had to hold tight to stay locked together. And in the middle of all the sliding and holding, of all the moving from side to side and up and down, I kissed her breast and found myself with a wonderful buttermilk taste in my mouth.

We were indoors again. She sat on the edge of the sofa and leaned against me and I wished that I lived inside her. But her folks would be home soon. I pulled on my clothes. The air in the small room seemed close and heavy from our bodies and I wondered if her mother would notice. I looked hard at the room, trying to soak up the details, wanting to remember it years from now. I savored the stillness and the dark, I savored the warmth of the heater and the glow of the grate. I savored the buttermilk. I savored Yvonne.

When Yvonne came back into the room I was standing there with the five-dollar bill in my hand. She was dressed, fresh and soft. For a moment she didn't see the money. I hadn't meant for her to see it, honest to God I hadn't. I had remembered that it was in my watch pocket and I had pulled it out to look at it, wondering why I had ever put it there in the first place. Don't ask me why I did it, I just did. So I stood there, a simple fool, feeling the blood in my face and watching Yvonne turn to stone.

I think she saw the money from across the room but it didn't really hit her, didn't really register, until she was standing in front of me. But she saw it then, for certain.

"Oh, God," she said, "oh, God, you've ruined it. You've ruined it. Oh, God . . ."

Her voice trailed away and the tears came, pushed down her face by deep, throbbing sobs. I reached out to her. She stepped backward, quickly, sharply, not wanting me to touch her, not wanting my hand to contaminate her, not wanting to admit that I was alive. And I probably wasn't. She was trying hard to choke off the sobs, to stop the tears. She wasn't going to cry for me.

There was nothing else I could do. I *was* a fool. I *had* ruined it. I opened the door, the awful dampness and cold cutting through me at once. I knew I had to leave but I didn't want to and I kept trying to think of something to say, something that would explain the five-dollar bill. But the miracle didn't happen. I was speechless again.

"Wait."

It was not a request, it was a command and I turned in the doorway, half gladly, half warily, the tone of her voice shaking me. She walked to the door and stood in front of me, her face flat and unfeeling, her eyes dark solid points of hardness. She held out her palm.

"Give it to me. Give it to me. It's mine. I earned it. I can do whatever I want with it."

She was standing there, demanding her rightful pay, a price negotiated in advance and brought with me in the watch pocket of my jeans. I pushed the five-dollar bill toward her. Very slowly she reached for it, gently curled her fingers around the bill, increasing the pressure until she was squeezing the paper with white knuckles. Then in a smooth, furious motion she jerked her arm backward, ripping the bill from my hand.

"From now on," she hissed, "you don't have the price. You'll *never* have the price again!"

I didn't go to school for two days, and when I did Yvonne wasn't there. After school I walked in the cold and dim light down past Yvonne's house. I could see the railing where we sat and I wondered if there were buttermilk stains on the boards. There were no lights on.

The narrow highway was empty and I shuffled on the pavement past the tiny rough-plank garage where Yvonne's brother parked his old Chevrolet. The doors were open and I could see the grill of the car grinning out at me. I felt uneasy, walking past Yvonne's house like that. I didn't belong there; she had made that clear. I stopped in the middle of the highway, intending to go back. Before I could move I heard the engine of the Chevrolet grind into life. The car rolled forward and turned in my direction on the road. It stopped, the engine idling. I figured Yvonne's brother was going to Kermit. I wondered if he would mind giving me a lift. But I didn't wonder long. The car's gears pounded and it lurched forward, the engine racing. Straight at me.

The whole thing didn't register. The car didn't have the lights on and the distance fooled me. I stood there almost too long before I leaped sideways, diving onto the gravel. As I rolled over the car raced by and I caught a glimpse of the driver. It was Yvonne. I got up and stared down the highway until I couldn't see the car anymore. And I knew then that she was gone for good.

It was dark when I got back to my shed. I fumbled trying to open the door. Something caught my eye and I lit a kerosene lamp. A five-dollar bill was nailed in the center of the door. The nail was a railroad spike, driven straight through the face on the bill and through the door, two inches of the rusty iron sticking through into my room.

❄

SPRING

Chapter 16

I couldn't be sure, but now and then the sky got a darker blue tone to it and the wind seemed to slow to a gentle breeze, carrying just a hint of something warm from wherever it came. There were no buds on the trees yet or anything, but winter was dying and maybe it would be possible soon to swim in the river again, or walk in the woods with my shirt off or just lie in the sun at the edge of a cane field. At least it was getting close enough to think about.

Spring in Crum never came gently. It was raw in its early days, refusing to allow anyone to let down his guard against the blowing rain. The stoves in the houses still glowed and the coal dust still filtered into the living rooms and parlors.

I sat in my shed thinking about Genna and about how men came in through the front door. There was no fire in the wood stove in the kitchen and the shed was so cold I wrapped a blanket around me and thought about that a lot — about courage and being afraid. And I thought maybe I was afraid. It was not easy admitting that, but at least I thought of something to do about it.

Off the upriver end of the schoolground there was a cemetery. In all the time I lived in Crum I never saw a funeral held there, but old people would come and clean the graves and the place looked cared for, used, if you know what I mean. Sometimes in the sad light of evening I would see a stooped form pulling weeds or picking up twigs around the grave markers. Maybe the graveyard was haunted, maybe not. But it sure was lonely.

Strangely, sometimes I liked to pay a visit to it. Especially on those days when Crum was closing in around me and I was having trouble breathing. It was one of the few places where there were people who had gotten out, had gotten away from Crum.

Now, I waited in that graveyard for the sun to go down. If I really was a man, if I really could do things that I was afraid of, I could sit in a graveyard until the sun went down and then walk through it in the dark. But it had to be really dark, black dark, dark like there never would be any more light again, before I would allow myself to leave. That's what I had decided.

I had picked a smooth grave, a plot of ground that hadn't sunk below the original level of the earth after the burial dirt had settled. The old plots were all like that — as though the grave diggers never quite put back enough dirt to make it back to ground level. But I had picked a good flat one, and my back rested against the gravestone.

As the light faded my mind began to fill up. I imagined haints — Appalachian ghosts — hiding behind the stones. My head became packed with fear and I felt my throat contract with panic. I wasn't trying to prove anything to anyone else — just to me. I didn't dare move a muscle, because if I did in an instant I'd be up and running, splitting the new grass of spring like the star halfback on the best football team in the county. But I didn't run. I sat there, with my mouth dry, imagining ghosts in the trees and waiting for total darkness.

It never came. Before the sun went down, the moon was already on the way up. Either that or I fell asleep. I sometimes do that when I am really frightened; I get so tensed up that I suddenly drop off. A year or so before I was down at the river just fooling around when it occurred to me that I had never really spent any time on the Kentucky side. I had been on the Kentucky shore lots but I had never camped on Kentucky soil. It looked just like the West Virginia side, but knowing that it was Kentucky made it different, somehow. It was strange. I had never even seen a house on that side of the river, and for all I knew those Kentucky pig fuckers who threw rocks at us and shot us out of our coal boat lived in caves. I went home and got my gunny sack, a couple of cold potatoes from a pot on the stove and my best blanket. I was going to sleep in Kentucky.

I settled on a thick stand of trees at the edge of the river, in undergrowth so dense that I had to get down and crawl,

belly to the ground, to get inside it. Anybody trying to get to
me while I was asleep in that thicket would make so much
noise coming in that they were bound to wake me up. I ate the
potatoes and watched the light turn to gray and then finally
the night soaked up the river until it wasn't there any more. I
could hear it, but I couldn't see it. I was alone — just like in
the cemetery.

Somewhere in the night I heard voices. They were moving toward me. Small tree limbs snapped and brush was pulled
aside. There were three or four guys, and they had come down
to the river for the night. They built a small fire and settled
down less than five yards from my blanket. They talked in very
low tones, almost whispers, but now and then I heard small
bits of their conversation. They were going to fish. They were
going to fish all night. About the only thing you were ever
going to catch out of the Tug River was a carp or two, or maybe
catfish, but then actually catching a fish was never the reason
anyone around here went fishing. You went fishing to go fishing. At least, that's what we did. It made me feel strange knowing that Kentucky boys did exactly the same thing. And then
I heard the distinctive snick of a rifle bolt being worked, and
I knew that at least one of them had a gun.

I was wide awake, but I hadn't moved. I was trying to
figure out what to do. If I didn't get out of that thicket I would
be in a hell of a fix if one of those guys decided to burn some
of it, or if the moon came out and they saw me, or if I farted
or sneezed or just plain belched. On the other hand, if I did
manage to sneak out and those Kentucky boys saw me running, there would be hell to pay. So what the fuck could I do?
I was trapped. And in the middle of forcing my mind to deal
with it, in the middle of trying to figure out whether I could
break from the thicket and run to the river and get across
without getting a .22 slug in my butt — I fell asleep.

When I woke up it was late morning, the sun was high,
the Kentucky boys were gone, their fire dead and the ashes
barely warm, and I was still rolled snugly in my blanket.

I don't know if I fell asleep this time or what, but it never
got dark. I waited, waited much longer than I had intended to

wait. But it never happened. Up through the branches of the trees the stars kept popping out, supporting the feeble light of the moon. There was always enough light to make me stay, but not enough light to keep me from being afraid. Finally I got up and walked as slowly out of that graveyard as I have ever walked out of anything. And I kept walking, step by careful step, until I got to the road. I turned and looked back at the gravestones glowing a little in the thin light, the branches of the trees making beckoning signals to me in the light breeze. I had gotten out of there by walking slowly and steadily but it had never been completely dark so I hadn't proved a thing. Besides, I knew it would never work with Crum. To get out of Crum would have to be an act of surgery, a falling ax on an outstretched limb. To get out of Crum I would have to bolt, quickly and efficiently, severing everything at once.

I looked again at the graveyard. It really wasn't scary or haunted at all. Mostly it was dead grass and rotting flowers, fallen-over grave markers and worn-down stones. The river had risen over it a couple of times in the past twenty years and most of the debris still hadn't been cleared out. And all the people there were dead. It really was a sad sight but not much to be afraid of.

My bladder ached for release and I took a leak there on the side of the little dirt road, pissing in the direction of the graveyard.

Chapter 17

There should have been something more special about this, but there wasn't. There should have been more ceremony, more of something that makes good memories. But there wasn't. I had looked forward to this day for such a long time, actually counting the months or the weeks or the days trying to hurry the whole thing so that I would wake up some morning and it would be over.

The last day of school. The last day I would spend in Crum High School.

It's just that sometimes I thought it would never come and I thought that if it ever did come it would be something special, something to remember, something to really enjoy. But it wasn't. There was something about it that was dull and ordinary, boring. It was like all the other days.

For a long time, for years, I had thought about this particular last day of school. I was stuck in a school that was hardly a school and I knew that there must be something beyond that, but I didn't know what it was. All I knew was that I had to go looking for it. I always thought that the last day would be the one that would taste good, the one that would make me feel liberated. I would spend the day running up and down the hallways, kicking doors and generally being a goddamn fool, delirious with my new freedom. But it was not that way at all.

I felt something all right, but it wasn't what I wanted. For one thing, kids didn't seem to be acting any differently. They seemed a little too normal, a little too much like it was any other school day. It was almost as though they didn't care one way or the other that school was in or school was out, it didn't matter. Some of them even seemed to be sad, as though they were sorry that it was over. Sorry — I couldn't understand that.

A couple of the kids who rode the bus came up and shook my hand. They lived far downriver and knew that they would not be seeing me during the summer, and also knew that this was my last year and if I had my way they wouldn't ever see me again. Everybody sort of knew that I planned to get out, but there was never any real plan about that, no day that anybody could point to and say it was going to be the last day in Crum for me. The whole idea just sort of hung there.

There were some ceremonies on that last day, teachers awarding kids certificates for best reader, or speller, or whatever. An award to the kid who had read the most books, another to the best math student. I didn't win any. But it didn't matter. Throughout the whole day, I felt apart from all those little prizes.

Elly stopped me in the hallway and kissed me. She really hung one on me, her tongue working as she ground her hips into mine. She had never done anything like that right out in the open at school before. And she made sure that her timing was right — Ruby was standing right next to us when Elly let me have it. The truth is, though, once Ruby knew I was really going to leave, she pretty well forgot about me. She concentrated on Mule instead.

I thought about Yvonne and how she should be here. She would have gotten some of those awards for sure — especially for the most books read. And she would have been dressed up in a dress that none of us would have seen before, and she would have been beautiful.

All day long I kept waiting for something unexpected. I felt listless instead of excited. And then I figured it out. A lot of times the worst thing in your life can be the focus of your life, your whole reason for getting through another day, and you miss it, even if you didn't like it, when it's gone. It must have been that way with me and Crum, and the school was a central part of that. I had beaten the school, I had gotten it over with, and I was, at least, half out of Crum because of that. And it was a letdown. I had lost half of my drive, my focus, the intense dislike that was my reason for waking up for another day. Crum. I felt sort of like the western gunfighter who looks for years for the bad guys who shot his brother, or whomever. And then he finds them and he kills them. And what is there left for him to do after that?

I got my certificate that proved I had completed Crum High School. They handed them out at noon.

Sometime in the middle of the afternoon, when no one was paying attention, before the official end of the last school day, before the final ceremony, I cut down a side hallway, out a back door, went past the putrid outhouses, jumped over the bank, slid down to the river bottom and took off through an old cane field.

SUMMER . . . AGAIN

Chapter 18

It was early morning and hotter than hell and I woke before daylight. The night temperature must have stayed near ninety and now Mattie had put a fire in the stove and I guess breakfast was underway. The back of the stove that stuck into my sleeping shed made a furnace out of the place and I knew that in a matter of minutes I would be driven out.

I got up and pulled on my shirt. The pants I was sleeping in were soaked with sweat, so I took them off and threw them outside. Under my bed was my flour sack with a couple of potatoes, a piece of cured bacon that I had laid in from the meat robbery, and some salt. I tied up the end of the sack, then tied the whole thing in a loop with a short piece of rope so that it would hang over my shoulder. I got some matches and my pocket knife, scrambled around in the darkness for my jeans, left the shed and began to climb Shit Hill. The early mountain light began to filter through the trees.

I waited on the side of the hill for a minute or two, as I always did, hoping the place would burn down, but nothing happened. Higher up the hill I could begin to see out over the valley and catch sight of other ridges falling away across the river and into Kentucky, each ridge like the other. The light was coming stronger and the sack felt comfortable over my shoulder and I liked the tired feeling that came as I pushed up the hill. I cut over to my left and made an open space where I could look down and see the school. When I got there I knew it was a mistake. I was done and I really didn't want to see that school again. I wanted to see something else that day.

I left the open and went back into the woods. As many times as I had been up on Shit Hill, I never really had been to the actual *top* of it, never really had seen what was on the other side, although I knew it could only be other ridges, standing in ranks as they measured off from the river valley. I decided to go look. My climb was easy. Shit Hill wasn't a real mountain, anyway, just a long sloping ridge that was a little too steep for houses and farming. It was bright full daylight by the time I reached the top of the hill, the top of the ridge.

I couldn't see a damn thing. The trees were so thick that any hope of seeing the valley — or what lay beyond — was completely cut off. I should have realized it, of course, but then a kid who climbs to the top of the hill, any hill, has a right to expect to see something. But you couldn't see anything, even from the top.

I walked the ridge. It was still early morning and I felt good and I wondered why I had never taken the trouble to come up here before. The woods really were beautiful, up where people had not gotten around to cutting them. Oh, I suppose they had been torn up at some time in the past, but that was a long time ago and the woods were looking good again. I found some nut trees and told myself that I would come back in the autumn to gather the nuts.

I was walking in a general upriver direction, the ridge running parallel to the river valley, and I thought I would just keep walking and see where I came out. The air was even warmer now, but sweet and thick with the aroma of the woods. About an hour later I came to a huge outcropping of rocks. The trees just came up to them and stopped and the tops of the rocks reached away through the branches. They bulked up on my right, holding off the vegetation that grew against them, finally breaking out into the light to overlook the valley. I decided to climb to the top and have a look, even though I was never too crazy about rock climbing. Snakes loved the warm rocks and almost always you could find one lounging around in a crack somewhere, baking his shiny body in the heat. But the thought of a view of the valley pushed me on.

The climb wasn't hard. The rocks lay in an easy jumble, boulder on boulder, lots of good footholds. It was like climbing a ladder. At the top, I thought for a minute I was going to be disappointed again, not be able to see, since brush grew there in the cracks and deposits of earth that had collected over hundreds of years. But then I came out on one particular rock, one that jutted far out beyond the leaves and the brush, beyond the tangle of vines and little plants. I could see the valley and I could see the river, the railroad tracks, the highway, and I could see Crum.

It was beautiful. The sun was directly overhead, flooding the valley with a sort of liquid illumination caused by the heat and the shimmer from the valley. The scene was more than I had ever known to look for. It was like a perfect toy. The lanes of the town were perfectly straight and didn't have a bump in them. The river was crisp and sharp, a deep green color that looked pure and wholesome. The tiny houses on each side of the highway were put there by elves who were laying out a village around which to build a fairy tale. I couldn't believe it. I stared at the scene until my eyes hurt.

Later I got hungry and I took some very dry twigs and built a small fire, just large enough to cover a couple of the potatoes. When it had produced some good embers I raked the coals aside, put the potatoes on the rock where the fire had been, then put the coals back into place. While the potatoes were baking I took out the bacon, sliced it into thick strips and jammed them on the end of a sharp stick. When I thought the potatoes had cooked long enough I took a small stick, sharpened the end, and shoved it into a potato. The stick went in easily and I knew they were just about done, so I held the bacon over the last of the coals until it was crisp. I ate it, all of it, and I can never remember food that was any better. The potato skins were black and crisp and I cracked them apart and ate the soft, steaming, white pulp along with great bites of bacon. I built the small fire back up and I chewed and looked at the scene below, looked at that smooth highway again, gracefully curving beyond my vision. When the food was gone I let the fire die down, grow cold, then scattered the ashes with my hands.

I lay on the rock and stared down at the town, trying to find out what was going on. Somewhere down there Homer Wiley was feeding his game cocks, the tough little fighting chickens that the law had been trying to lay their hands on. And Tyler Wilson was going back to his store after lunch. Genna Prince was probably looking out her front window, wishing somebody would come in and rescue her from Clyde, only nobody would because Clyde was the constable and he could shoot people.

A snake moved lazily into the sunshine and looked at me, puzzled. I picked up a large stick and took aim, only it was a small snake and at the last minute I changed my mind. I don't know what kind of snake it was but it didn't seem interested in bothering me, so I figured what the hell, and just smacked the stick on the rock. He crawled away, unafraid.

By this time, half the houses in town would have pots of pinto beans on their stoves, with potatoes peeled and ready to fry and pork side meat sliced on the drainboard next to the sink. Nip's mother would be boiling water to get it hot enough to put into the wash tub, hot enough to make the sulfur scum form on the top so she could scoop it off before she put her clothes in. Doors on outhouses would be opening and closing and people would be hitching up their pants and pulling down their skirts. Nip and Mule were probably wondering where I was, a little curious but probably not really caring. I would be back. And then I knew that when I left Crum I would never see either of them again. There was something so very final about that, something that was all part of the deal and yet something I had never really thought about before. The truth was, once I left, I might never see *anybody* from Crum again, not just Mule and Nip, but Oscar and Mattie and Elvira and even Ethan Piney. But somehow it was Mule and Nip that kept coming into my mind, their images dancing in the sunlight that ribboned through the trees. Tears came. I didn't plan it that way, but the tears just came.

Mule had always been a sort of mystery to me. He was my best friend, a guy I could count on for as long as I lived. But sometimes not. Often he stood back waiting for me to do something, to get into something. He'd wait to see what it was that he wanted to do about it, if anything. It was sort of like the time in Tyler's store when everybody knew that Clyde was going to pound my ass. Mule was there, but he wasn't really involved. Nobody hit Mule; they only hit me. But in a town where there weren't that many people, you had to have some friends, and I guess Mule was a friend.

Nip was different. I think if I had asked Nip to stuff his pockets with rocks and jump into the river, told him that I needed for him to do that, he would have done it. Nip was little and he was always hanging around and he couldn't run as fast as the rest of us and he wasn't as strong, and I don't know why such things as those kept him out of the best friend category whenever I was thinking about best friends. He *was* a best friend, really. And up there on that hillside I realized that I might never see my best friends again.

"I'm leaving! I'm leaving!" Suddenly I shouted it out. Then I said it to myself, and then over and over aloud, until tears streamed down my face.

"I'M LEAVING! I'M LEAVING! I'M LEAVING!"

The sounds died away across the valley and I felt sad and I was alone again. I turned my face into the breeze so that if any more tears did come I could convince myself that the wind caused them. I sat back down on the rock and pulled my legs up against my chest. My eyes closed and I rocked slowly back and forth. I grew drowsy and lay back on the rock and went to sleep. I woke up to the fading light and looked again at the town below. It was in deep shadow now and only a few lights showed where the houses were. It was too nice up here, Crum looked nice and it would just make my decision too hard, to look at Crum and find it beautiful.

Chapter 19

It was three o'clock in the afternoon of a stifling day in early August and I was going down to the river to say goodbye and to get my brains beat out.

It was a ritual. I wouldn't have called it that then — it didn't come to me until many years later — but it was a ritual and there was no escaping it. There had been one at each stage of my life in Crum and there would be one, now, when I left. There was no way out. But if I was going down to the river to get my ass kicked, by God at least they were going to have to work at it. This time they were going to have to pull out all the stops.

The stench of the river found me before I found it. With the water down to only waist deep in most places, the sluggish stream simply could not carry the load of garbage piled up along the banks.

At least six different guys had stopped by the house to ask me to come down to the river for a swim. They knew it was my last day in Crum and they wanted to make sure I got a proper send-off. The bastards were there now. I could hear them splashing and shouting, the noises ringing sharp, loud, through the heat that layered the valley. I knew they would be spread out, each waiting to be the first to see me as I topped the rise of the river bank, each wanting to be the first to fall silent and to settle down in the water.

Well, screw them. I was scared and they were the reason for my fear and I have always hated things that frightened me for no good reason. I didn't know about rituals, so I didn't know then that they didn't understand what they were doing, either. I topped the rise of the river bank and half-galloped down the slope. I pasted a large grin across my face, waded into the water, and floated and pushed my way out toward the middle.

Time slowed down. The sun beat on the surface of the river and reflected back into my face, and I could feel the heat on my shoulders and back as I moved into the water. The river was hardly flowing fast enough to make noise and the others in the river were silent for a minute or so. There were no clouds in the sky. It was one of those Appalachian August days when the heat is so intense that nothing moves, and everything bakes that's caught in the narrow river valleys. It was one of those days where just opening your eyes makes your forehead sweat.

The others were nearer the Kentucky side, lounging around the large rock that was our diving platform. Four of them sat on the top, three more bobbed around in the slow current. The water was about chest deep at most and the shallow parts just came up to my knees.

I had spent the last week selling everything I owned, everything except my old rifle. I sold the stuff quietly, trying not to stir up questions, holding off the poking and prying that I knew would come if word got around. But the word did anyway, and so now I was going to have to beat it out of there before I had planned, just bug out without telling anybody. Slip away. Just me and an old cardboard suitcase.

I forgot about the ritual, but it didn't forget me. And here we were in the stinking Tug River, seven bodies and a victim.

Things started pleasantly enough. It actually was sort of nice. Of course, nobody said "sorry to see you go" or anything like that. But then, guys didn't do that. We were just sort of loafing there, us guys who had known each other for all those years, just lollygagging around in the river, letting the sun beat down and the river wash up and talking about all those things that were usually talked about, like we'd done a thousand times.

Ott Parsons was there, his big mouth spouting cuss words and streams of river water. He was trying to climb on the rock and the others were pushing him off. It was funny to watch Ott haul his big frame out of the water, get about halfway up the rock, begin to lose his balance, and then be nudged off by Nip, the smallest guy in the bunch. Ott was enjoying it, or he wouldn't have let people push him. He made a hell of a splash when he hit the water.

I was standing clear of the action, just letting things slide by, when Ott took a particularly spectacular fall and landed near me. His arm went out as he came down, grazing my shoulder and knocking me off balance. I laughed, just a little, and then waited for his next move because I felt sure there would be one. Instead, he splashed around in the pool and then made another try on the rock. The atmosphere was getting more strained. They all knew, I think, that the next time they looked I was going to be gone, and it was these guys — my friends — I was leaving. They didn't know what to say, and formal goodbyes were out of the question. The only thing left was to pretend that it really didn't make any difference, that I didn't really count for anything and to pick a fight with me to prove it. Of course, to *really* prove it I had to lose the fight, and since they knew I wouldn't lose on purpose, they were going to have to throw someone against me who they knew could do the job. That would be Ott.

A few minutes later a game of horse started in the river. Ott and I were the horses. We pulled and shoved for a few minutes, then I lost my balance and my rider, Nip, and I fell under. As we came up, Ott was shouting that the losers get another ducking and he made a grab for me. Except maybe for Cyrus Hatfield, Ott was the strongest guy in Crum and he had the bluff on every guy there. None of us thought we could lick him and, as a result, nobody tried. He pretty much got his way and we never crossed him up much, at least not so that he could figure out who did it. If you got the best of him in a wrestling match, he would get mad and start throwing punches. Ott won in the end, one way or another.

So Ott was the man chosen to do it, to goad me into a fight and to lick me. When he grabbed me it wasn't friendly. He meant to have the advantage from the very beginning and get it over with. I was really scared of Ott, but I was mad, too, and I didn't really want to get licked in front of all those guys. Ott tried to shove my head under water and that scared me even more, so I began to wrestle, to resist in earnest. I knew that I wouldn't throw a punch except as a last resort — if I threw a punch first, that meant that Ott would be free to do the same, and I was still clinging to the hope that I could get out of this without swapping punches.

I took a deep breath, gathered my legs under me, shoved upwards with most of my strength and then, when I felt him resist the upward thrust, I dropped all my weight and sank under water and out of his grasp, slipping his bear hug with hardly any effort. I bobbed to the surface and immediately faced him. The others didn't make a sound. The victim had been baited and the punishment had been chosen and there was nothing to do now but to sit and watch.

Ott let out an embarrassed laugh. He hadn't counted on losing me so fast and it didn't do much to make him look good. He made a dive for me and got one of my arms and I twisted to the side to avoid his full weight. As he threw himself forward he launched himself in the water and it was easy to drag his weight to the side as I twisted again. His grip on my arm began to hurt like hell, and I grabbed his hand to try to pry it off. That was a mistake. He got my other arm then and began to twist it, grunting as the struggle got a little tougher. We were both wrestling in deadly earnest now, no more tight smiles or tense laughs. And I knew we were getting down to it when I twisted to the side again and escaped one of Ott's hands — because he balled up a fist and smashed me full in the mouth.

The blood and salt flooded my mouth and nose and I spat to clear it away. Ott was standing there, lining up the next punch, and I looked at him through the tears that were coming now. As he drew back his arm I raised my foot free of the hip-deep water and kicked him in the chest. It was a move I had been practicing ever since I had seen a soldier do it in one of Coach Mason's war movies and it paid off. Ott was taken completely by surprise and I was able to punch him twice and kick him once more before he recovered.

It was like banging on a wall. I couldn't make a dent in him. We grabbed, gouged, kicked, punched and clawed each other for a full five minutes, standing and slipping there in the river, halfway between two states, blood running from wounds as scraps of cloth from our pants floated away in the current. The battle stirred up great clouds of sand and muck from the bottom and made the fight seem more dramatic than it actually was.

Ott had one major task — to force my head underwater, to actually shove it under. If he could control the situation long enough to do that, then I would have to give up and he would clearly be the winner and I would be beaten. I tried to keep him from doing it and I almost succeeded, but in the end he was a better fighter and stronger, and I got locked into his grasp and couldn't get out again. He began to bend me toward the water. I resisted with everything I had but I knew I was going to lose. All I wanted to do at that point was to make it cost him as much as possible. As I was forced over I managed to reach down between and through my legs and grab a solid handful of Ott's crotch. I couldn't tell what I really had hold of, but I wasn't going to let go. I squeezed and pulled, trying to rip out anything that was growing there. Amazingly, Ott did not let go of me. He knew that if he did, he might not be able to get me in such a position again. He nearly had me. As he bent my head another inch toward the water I pulled on his crotch all the harder and he gasped. I knew that I had a handful of something that counted. I was trying my goddamnedest to pull his dick and balls out and float them downriver like Ralph's dog.

I had to hand it to the sonofabitch, he didn't quit. He just kept bending and I just kept pulling and I knew that he was going to be able to duck me before I could twist his balls off. It was about then that I became aware that the other guys were yelling for Ott to beat me, to bust me, to do something, to do anything. As my face neared the water I looked to see who was leading the yelling, or maybe who wasn't yelling at all. And the guy making the most noise, the guy yelling hardest for Ott to kick my ass, that guy was Mule.

It didn't occur to me until then that they couldn't see that I had Ott by the crotch. My part of the action was under the muddy water and they just couldn't know what was going on. Damn them, I thought. Damn them! I can't even show them that I have the bastard by the balls, that I have him as much as he has me, and there never will be any way that I can prove it. My head was only inches away from the water now and I could hear the crying in Ott's breathing. He was really hurting, but so was I and I couldn't resist much longer. I only hoped the bastard wouldn't drown me.

My head went under — for a second. I guess I didn't realize it, what with all the grunting, straining and pulling, but my head went under and I drew in a noseful of water. I felt it going into my nostrils and I managed to stop it just short of my throat. If I coughed I was done for. Suddenly the back of my head was above water again, and Ott was loosening his grip. My God, I thought, he's going to settle for pushing my face under! I must have a better hold than I thought! As Ott let go I ducked fully under the water, twisted around so that I was facing him and, still holding onto his crotch, pulled with all my might — and then shoved.

I broke the surface and stood up. I had had my beating. He got me underwater. I was a mess, I ached and I pained and I didn't think I would be able to get out of the river by myself. But strangely enough I felt pretty good about the whole thing. Because there was Ott, puking his brains out.

Ott had lost face. He had licked me, but it had been a tough job and, if I knew what I knew, some of the other guys would be looking at him with some new thoughts in their heads. They were all quiet now, taking it all in and not making a commitment one way or the other. I knew mentally they were probing Ott, weighing new perspectives. Ott was going to have to build his reputation, if he could, all over again.

But he wouldn't build it on me. I looked at Ott, bent over the water, still gagging and holding both hands below the surface around his aching balls. I moved in closer, carefully, not wanting to fall into a trap. His agony was real. He didn't care where I was, or whether I was there at all. But I was. I lined myself up carefully and cocked my right hand. I slammed the punch into the side of his face as hard as I could, screaming at the top of my lungs as the fist cracked into his jaw and teeth. The punch spun him away from me facedown into the water. For a second or two no one moved, and then a couple of the guys jumped off the rock and grabbed Ott. When they pulled him out of the water blood was running from his mouth and he was still gagging on his puke.

I had been beaten, sort of. At least Ott had pushed my face under the muddy water. But Ott was the one who was sick. Ott was the one whose face was bleeding. Ott was the one who had to be pulled out of the river. So why the hell was everyone acting like I had done something wrong? It pissed me off. It really did. So I wanted more, I wanted a piece of those bodies on that rock who had watched the whole thing, who had participated with such certainty. I wanted a chunk of them and I wanted it now and I was going to get it.

They knew the fight was over and there was no longer any reason to hang around. They slid off the rock and moved toward shore. I pulled myself together a little and followed them. No one spoke. There was nothing to say. They just started to go home. Nip had gotten out of the river already. He was on the bank, squatting in the sun, his arms wrapped around his knees. I hadn't seen him, but he must have been there from before the fight. Then as we moved toward shore I saw Mule. Mule — sort of one of my best friends — had been yelling just a couple of minutes before as hard as anyone for Ott to kick my ass, to knock my fucking head off. Mule would do just fine, I thought. Mule would do just fine.

A couple of the guys were already to the bank and were climbing the sandy slope out of the river. On his feet now, Ott moved slowly up the bank. I was next and Mule was right behind me. I climbed for a few steps, maybe seven or eight, then paused until I could feel that Mule was going to pass me. I eased carefully to my right so that he would have to pass on my left. And as he drew even with me I turned and threw a right that caught him on the side of the head, a solid whack that resounded across the river. Mule dropped like a rock and rolled to the edge of the water, turned himself over slowly and rose to his knees. He was wobbly and surprised and even afraid. He looked at me as though I were crazy — this wasn't part of the game, the game was over. No one else moved or spoke, three of them still in the river, the others above me on the river bank. I backed off a couple of steps to make sure that no one could move behind me and then I waited. Sure as hell, I was going to be in for it now but I didn't really care. I was full of my new strength and confidence, I had issued a fresh challenge, and now I waited.

Some of them stared stupidly at me, the others stared stupidly at Mule. There was no movement, no sound, no nothing, just the bank and the river and the motionless bodies. Mule regained his feet slowly, the right side of his face swollen, the redness accentuated by the sun. He stumbled slowly past me up the bank, walked into a cane field and was gone. The others turned and followed and I was left alone with the river running a few yards away and the breeze rattling through the cane field. I had lost and I had won and I was confident and I was afraid. But most of all I was alone, just alone.

The others stood at the top of the bank now, and they looked back at me below them.

"Fuck you," one of them said. And they turned and were gone.

Chapter 20

There was an old cardboard suitcase in a closet in the house and I waited for Mattie and Oscar to go out to a revival meeting and I went in and took it. It wasn't much of a suitcase and I thought about just taking my gunny sack, but I felt that anybody going on the road should have a suitcase. Made them look a little less hillbilly, I thought. It was not my suitcase though and I felt strange about that, so I left my single-shot rifle there in its place as payment. If it were not for me the suitcase probably never would have been used again anyway, but somehow, knowing that Oscar would have the rifle made me feel good, or at least made me feel better. I loved Mattie and Oscar and that rifle was the best thing that I had ever owned.

I remembered a conversation Oscar and I had had the week before. I was rinsing off out by the well, a fresh bucket of water sitting on the board by the wellbox. I was taking dippers of the fresh, cool water and splashing them over my head and shoulders. Oscar came out and hung around for a few minutes, like he wanted to talk to me but didn't know what to say. He took the tin drinking dipper from the nail where it hung on the side of the wellbox and got himself a drink from the bucket.

"They's hirin' a few new men at the Number Seven. Mighten be a good place for you to start."

I heard what he said, but I didn't know how to answer. Good old Number Seven. Jesus, Oscar had spent half his life in that mine, in that dark hole in the ground, never seeing sunlight, breathing that black dust. Just the thought of doing that scared the hell out of me. I don't know how anybody did it — men will do anything to feed their families.

I had read that in the West they gave real names to the coal mines and the gold mines and the silver mines, names like Red Lady, Silver Queen, Leonard's Lode, Ruby Chief, Hungry Mother and Jokerville. But in West Virginia, they just gave them numbers. Good old Number Seven.

I didn't know how to answer. I mumbled something about, thanks, I'd probably like that, or something like that, a total lie. And Oscar knew it.

"Well," he said, "when yore ready to go and talk to `em about it, you let me know. I go with ye." And he turned and walked away.

Oscar took a few steps and then stopped, but he did not turn around. He stood there, looking out over Crum, his broad shoulders sagging a little. He said something, softly.

"I didn't hear," I said.

He still did not turn around. "I said, boy, don't go in the mines. Don't do whut I did. Don't go in the mines. I don't care how much money they offer you, boy, just don't you do it."

There was no one in the house when I took the suitcase, and I was grateful for that. I really didn't want to explain the cuts and bruises. And I didn't want to shake hands. My right hand was swollen and stiff and I had busted at least part of it on Mule's face. And I especially couldn't face Mattie. Maybe Oscar, but not Mattie. I had slept in her house — well, in a part of her house — and she would not understand why I wanted to leave it. She would think that I was ungrateful for what the two of them had done for me — or worse, that I didn't love them.

I put a few thing in the suitcase, mainly some clothes that I thought I might need. I also put in a belt knife that I had, a sharpening stone, and a sheath. I felt a little better, knowing that the knife was in there. It replaced the rifle. I also packed the one book that I owned. It was by Jules Verne and was called *The Mysterious Island*. Benny had stolen it from the school library, discovered that he couldn't read it, and given it to me. It was the only book that I had ever owned and I was sort of proud of it.

And I emptied the coffee can from under my bed. I had exactly thirteen dollars and thirty-seven cents. With that much money I could go anywhere.

So I threw my stuff in the suitcase, closed it, wrapped an extra leather belt around it and cinched it up as tight as I could, took off my clothes and flopped on the bed. The aches would keep on aching, but most of the bleeding had stopped.

I woke up just after first light, just before they started the fire in that stove, just before anybody else thought to go out into the day, just before my brain could tell the rest of me that what I was doing was jumping off the edge of the earth, just before my courage failed.

I walked down the hill with my suitcase and looked straight ahead. I didn't want accidentally to see something I liked and get that feeling that I thought I might get if I admitted to myself that I was really leaving — that I probably wouldn't see any of this trash again. So I looked straight ahead and went on down the hill, down to the highway by the railroad tracks, and I felt the day heat up on the back of my neck. I got to the highway and walked upriver a little way, to a spot on the road where a car could pull off if the driver wanted to stop. The only trouble with the spot was that I could see Ruby's house from there, and I didn't want that. I hadn't told her a thing and she hadn't asked. But maybe because I could see her house was why I went to the wide spot in the first place. I don't know.

Nip rode up on his rusted old bicycle. He must have been waiting on the highway somewhere, knowing that I would come down the hill. He rode up from behind and I didn't know it was him until he was right next to me. He went on by, then turned the bike and stopped across the road, off the pavement. He was pointed toward Kermit, the same way I was. I put the suitcase down and stood there, determined not to say anything, and a couple of years seemed to go by.

"I reckon you're leavin'," he finally said.

"Yeah. Reckon so."

"You done good with Ott. I thought he was agoin' to puke his innards out."

"Ott can go fuck hisself. I ain't got no more time for anybody like him. Nor Mule, neither."

We were just passing the time of day before we went down to the river to take a few shots at some floating garbage. Nip shifted on the bicycle seat.

"Bet you could lick him again, iffen you tried."

"Don't care. Ain't never goin' to see him again, anyway."

"Goin' to Williamson?"

"Don't know. Wherever."

"Got any money?"

"Some. What's it to you?"

"I've got four dollars, iffen you'd like to borry it."

"Don't need your money. Don't need anybody's money." I was uncomfortable. Nip was doing just what I tried to get away from, making me feel there was something to Crum, after all.

"Look, why don't you just git yourself and that bike out of here? Ain't nobody goin' to stop here with that bicycle over there. So why don't you just git?"

He slowly shifted his weight so that the bike was balanced and looked as though he were going to ride away. But he stayed put.

"There's some here that call you friend," he said quietly. And he reached up with his hand and rolled up the sleeve of his T-shirt. High up on his arm, right next to his shoulder, some short, white scars ran across his arm, scars I recognized from Ralph Parson's dog, the one we'd drowned.

"You done good with that dog."

"You don't owe me nuthin', nuthin' a'tall." I mumbled. I had not forgotten about the dog ripping into Nip's arm, but I had never seen the scars. I was going to cry.

"I know I don't owe you nuthin'. I paid you back." There was something odd about the way he said that. I couldn't put my finger on it.

"What? You paid me back? How'd you do that?"

"Well, I did, that's all. I jist did."

"Sure you did."

I was trying to be sarcastic, to be a smartass.

"You know when Clyde and them was a'beatin on you in the store, when they thought you had blowed up Clyde's shithouse? You know that? Well, when I knew they wuz a'goin to do that, I went and got Wade. Wade blowed up Clyde's shithouse, but it was me that blowed up Tyler's. I couldn't figure no other way to git them to let you go."

Oh, God. Oh, God. He was going to do it. He was going

to make me cry. He was going to make me walk across that road and pull his little ass off that bicycle and hug the shit out of him. He was going to make me try to talk him into going with me. He was going to make me feel like a human being. Like Crum was where I belonged.

"Big fuckin' deal. I didn't need yore help. I didn't need no help from nobody."

It was then a car slowed down. I didn't even thumb it down, it just stopped anyway about ten yards down the highway and the driver looked back through his rear window to make sure I was coming. I didn't move, just stood there looking at Nip on his bicycle. I felt my urge to travel rapidly fading away. The guy in the car tooted his horn but I still didn't move. The car's gears clashed and the engine revved up and I thought he was driving away. I picked up my suitcase. I could stay one more day. But the car was backing up. It damn near ran into me as I started across the road toward Nip. The car stopped between us and the guy leaned out the window. He looked pretty irritated. He said to get in, that he didn't have all day, and that if I was going to Kermit he would take me all the way. I stood there for a few long seconds, then I opened the door and got in.

Nip looked at me in the car. His face went a little hard, then a little soft. He turned the bicycle around, waited for a second or two, then rode in a couple of loose circles in the middle of the road. I knew that he would not stop riding again, that he would keep just circling in front of the car until he was ready and then he would ride away. And that's what he did. His little body pumped the pedals of the old bicycle and the sun burned into his back and he did not say a word all the time he rode there, around and around. He did not understand how I could say things like that and how I could get in that car. And I couldn't understand it, either. All I knew was that I had just cut some sort of tie, and I had used a rusty knife to do it. And then he rode away. He disappeared over a small rise in the road and I never saw him or Crum again.

LOOKING FOR BENNY

(Editor's note: As a young boy, Lee Maynard rode out of the town of Crum in a 1941 Chevrolet. They had to push the car to get it started. In the last line of his novel, *Crum*, Lee writes that he never saw Crum again. But he did. Many years later. There was something he had to look for . . .)

Looking for Benny

by Lee Maynard

Bull Mountain was supposed to rise in front of me, but it never did.

The road slid through the narrow valley and then rose only slightly and, before I was ready, I saw the Tug River Valley baking in the Sunday morning heat of an Appalachian August.

Bull Mountain was gone. It had been shaved off, pushed over the side of the hill, used to fill in a hollow or two. The whole aspect of the mountain had changed, more open now, more gentle. The mountain no longer guarded the approach to Crum, no longer loomed in the darkness as the narrow road from Wayne twisted up to the tiny pass at the top, widened briefly, and then fell away steeply down the mountain's flank and away into the Tug River Valley, carrying the road in a long, sweeping curve where we once rode heavy, fat-tired bicycles in a screaming descent without brakes. It wasn't a mountain any more. It was just a hill, a bump in the road to Crum, harmless, sleeping in the searing sun of a cloudless mid-summer Sunday morning. And there were no kids on bicycles, no kids with ragged jeans and dirty high-top tennis shoes. The road was empty.

Benny wasn't there.

I stopped the car and got out, breathing in the hot, rich mountain air and listening to the buzz of insects in the weeds beside the highway. I could see into the valley below and across the river into the ridges of Kentucky. The ridges looked dark and lush in the distance, and I wondered why I had never gone over there and hiked through them. But then, there were a lot of things I didn't do.

I don't know why I stopped the car there. Nothing was familiar to me. I must have been looking for something, but I didn't know what.

And then I realized the Mountaintop Beer Garden was

gone, that old and twisted building that once haunted the very top of Bull Mountain, that building smelling of stale beer and sweat, its windows cracked, a single naked light bulb over the door. That building where we were never allowed to go, the building of our favorite stories, the building of our fears. Of course it would be gone, gone with the top of the mountain, bulldozed and swept into some hollow where the smell of its beer-soaked floor would be forever buried in the forgotten history of West Virginia. Perhaps gone for decades before I stood here on the truncated top of what used to be Bull Mountain.

Suddenly I didn't want to be there. Not in the bright sun of the mountaintop, not on my way to Crum, not in Wayne County. I wanted out of there. I wanted to close my eyes and be gone. But things don't work that way. They didn't work that way when I lived in Crum, and they wouldn't — I knew — work that way now.

On some mysterious signal the insects fell quiet and I wondered at that incredible silence that can come over a hot summer day in West Virginia. You can hear the hush of mountains, and the clear scream of a hawk over the valley. You can hear forever. And I heard Crum below me and up the river. I could hear its heart beat. I had come here to see Crum, to find Benny, and so I drove on.

I came across a small rise and I saw the stone face of the high school rising out of the field, the football field crowded in between the building and the railroad track.

No. There was no football field there. Where I had chased and been chased, hit and been hit, where I learned left from right and right from wrong . . . there was a paved parking lot. The field was now solid, black and ugly, boiling in the sun in front of the old stone high school building and behind a high fence and a gate that gave off the clear message: keep the hell out. It was the football field where my father, Amos, was the first coach, where, in the first year we had a football team, we had fifteen players, fourteen uniforms and only thirteen pairs of football shoes. Some of us had to change shoes just to get into the game. I still have scars from being knocked into the rocks and gravel that littered that field. Before each game we would walk down the field and pick up the bigger pieces, throwing them toward the railroad tracks. But those rocks had lives of their own — they always came back to the football field, came back for me to fall on.

Now, the field was paved, open space for little kids given way to blacktop and a place for cars.

Behind the fence, at the edge of the pavement, cheap school buildings were scattered wherever they would fit, in no apparent order, with no apparent plan.

I drove the silent mile or so that it takes to get through town, past the small, white church across the tracks on my right, standing next to Bascomb Copley's old house. I didn't remember the church, but I did remember Bascomb's house, solid, brick, still sitting smack in the middle of Crum, still commanding everything it looked out on. In some quirk of fate, I had once lived directly behind that house, and then, later, directly in front of it, over a garage so near the tracks that passing trains made the glasses dance on the kitchen table. The garage was gone, burned, a rotting pile of blackened timbers marking the spot.

As I drove I noticed that every available flat space on the valley floor that I could see had a house — or something — on it. Every open area, every field in the tiny river bottom had been crowded, built, jammed shoulder to shoulder with small buildings, tiny houses. Crum had grown, and it had grown in the only places it could — in the open areas of the town, in the fields where we ran, chased by whomever we had offended at the moment, heading for the river down at the end of the lane past Ralph Dawson's white house at the edge of the bank, then headlong over the hill into the brush below, where we could lose anybody. Absolutely anybody. And Ralph was a good guy; when he saw us thundering by, he would cover for us. But most of the time he was with us, leading the way, running for his life.

At the upriver end of town I turned off the highway, crossed the tracks, and pulled up in front of a concrete block building where Bascomb's store used to be. The store had been a high, rambling wooden building that smelled good and seemed to lean slightly upriver. It was gone. The block building had no memories and no personality and would never take the place of Bascomb's store.

I remember the time Bascomb's grandson, Howard Copley, and I rode a hay truck into Bascomb's barn, near the store. We sat on top of the load and as a rafter went by Howard and I both reached up and grabbed it. The truck drove out from under us and we hung there, a full story above the hard packed dirt floor, swinging on the rafter, doing something we hadn't done before, laughing and yelling, having a right fine old time of it. Until we realized the truck wasn't coming back.

On the short drive through Crum I had seen not a single soul. I wanted to go somewhere, see *someone*, ask some questions, do *something*, maybe find Benny — but there was nothing to do. I waited for the sound of voices or the thump of running feet; I waited to hear the slam of a door or the creaking sound of a well pulley as the glistening bucket came up cool and dripping from the dark of the earth. I listened for sounds that were gone from my ears but were soaked into the hills around me and I knew they would be there if only I knew where to dig.

Briefly, fleetingly, I caught the smell of chicken frying and I tried to hold on to it for a moment, but couldn't. It went away as surely as I had gone from Crum.

I drove back across the tracks and upriver to see how far the town had grown in that direction. It hadn't. Crum had grown in houses, but it hadn't grown in size. It still began about where the high school was, and still ended at the bottom of the hill past the turnoff to Bascomb's store. I was out of town in less than a minute.

I turned the car and went back down the road, crossed the tracks again and eased along the narrow dirt lane toward the church, a lane that had been there as long as Crum had been. I drove past the narrow spot where I wrecked my sister's bicycle. I think I broke a rib in that wreck. For a couple of weeks I couldn't raise my right arm and I went around pretending that I was left handed. But I didn't tell anybody about the busted rib; it was nothing compared to what my sister did to me when she saw the damage to the bicycle.

I passed the church and then Bascomb's house and eased the car slowly past some houses that crowded the side of the lane.

The houses were neat and the yards were trimmed and I knew that the people who lived there were proud of those houses. A small sign on the fence in front of one of them said "The Maynards". I felt a small catch in my throat. I didn't remember any other Maynards living in Crum when I lived there. And all the Maynards in Wayne County, God bless 'em, are relatives, somewhere along the line. Even when they don't want to be. A man was sitting on the porch, reading a newspaper. I nodded. He nodded. And I kept going.

But I knew he was a relative. The first Maynard came to Wayne County in the early 1700s and dug himself into a small valley in the heart of the county along what was then called Kiah's Creek. Maybe it's still called Kiah's Creek. When I first learned that name I thought it was beautiful. I still do.

And Maynards have been there ever since.

One of my grandfathers died in the Civil War, died in a small firefight that took place only a few hundred yards from his house, somewhere near Kiah's Creek. We Maynards tended not to stray too far, even to get shot and die.

I wanted to get to the river, but I didn't know how. The lanes that ran off in that direction seemed so much smaller now, more narrow. They ran off close to houses and near fences and they seemed private. I stopped at the end of one and looked toward the river and saw a small boy out along the lane. He was looking at me and the big car I was driving and he didn't move. He stood motionless and silent in the center of the lane, a tiny symbol, a guardian, his feet spread and his hands jammed into his pockets. Benny would stand like that, just after he had done something outrageous or obscene and just before one of us would hit him. He would go down, but be up before we could hold him there, and then the hitting would be all his, dirty fists flying in our faces, dirty arms wrapping around our necks.

But I was fantasizing again. I knew the boy wasn't Benny. How could he be? Even Benny would have grown *some* after all these years. But the boy would be someone to talk to, I thought. I pulled the car into the lane. And he was gone.

Past the high school again, then back across the tracks and upriver, back to a small restaurant I had seen. It sat on the edge of the hill next to the highway, across from the church. It was roomy and clean and bright and on this Sunday morning three or four of the regulars, all men, were gathered for coffee. I wondered if I would recognize anyone, but I didn't. Even if they were boys I had known . . . it had been a long time.

The lady who ran the restaurant was gracious and friendly and the coffee was good. I sat alone at a table at the back, next to the window, looking across the tracks at the church. A small crowd was gathered now, dressed in their church clothes, waiting for services to start. There was something comforting about people waiting for church services to start, some feeling of warmth and security. I've never really had that feeling. I couldn't remember the last time I waited for church services to start.

I drank coffee and my mind wandered.

Where was Elmer Dillon? Tall and lanky and quick, handsome.

And Bobby Robert Frederick Lester. He used to give his name that way, when a teacher asked him. Had four names, he said. More than anyone else in Crum. Bob Lester, who could handle a football better than he would ever know.

And Howard Copley. Small, gentle, and somehow wiser than the rest of us. I could never figure that out. There was something Howard knew that we didn't. And he knew that we would never know.

And Ralph Dawson. Ralph could figure it out. No matter what. When the rest of us were running, Ralph was figuring. I wondered how long it had been since Ralph ran.

And where was Geneva Marcum? A complexion like honey, hair like warm midnight and a mind that put the rest of us to shame. She was a friend, but she never really hung out with us. At least not with me. She was too smart for that. Long after I left Crum I remembered Geneva as being one of the most beautiful girls I had ever known. I hoped she was happy.

And Eli Crum. A sage in the making if ever I saw one. I sat in the restaurant and tried to remember where Eli had lived, and I couldn't. Seemed as though he lived everywhere, there in Crum. Seemed as though Crum were his.

And David Varney. When we lived just behind Bascomb's

house on Teachers' Lane, David had lived just behind us. He was a year or two older, and much more grown up than we were. We were punks, sort of, but David never fit that mold. He was calmer, deeper. We were boys; David always seemed to be a man. He never did the things we did — at least, I never saw him do them. He never stole green apples, never cut across the fields, never tried to outrun the freight train. Maybe he did those things when we weren't around. I surely hope so.

And where was Benny Musser? Where was the guy who could get us all arrested just by standing in the middle of the highway with his pants down? Had they finally locked him up somewhere? Had they finally chased him out of town?

And then I remembered. There never had been a Benny Musser. I created him. I made him live and act and do things that will upset the people who still live in Crum — if any of them ever read my book. They won't like Benny Musser. But I do. In spite of all the other things he was, Benny was at least colorful. To say the least. When I lived in Crum I was trapped inside my own mind and I had to invent someone who could be in there deeper than I was, someone who never once, not in his whole life, let the town of Crum get to him, never let it lock him up. He didn't give a damn about Crum, but then he didn't give a damn about anything. For Benny, Crum just didn't exist. I really liked that boy. In another place and time Benny would have been a great lawyer. Or maybe a writer.

The sun was burning full into the valley now and suddenly the door of the church opened and some brightly dressed kids came running out, ahead of the preacher. My coffee cup was full and hot and I realized that the waitress had filled it, and I had been so lost in my mind and my memories that I hadn't noticed. I rubbed my eyes and stretched and watched the kids across the tracks. I wondered if any of them were the kids of Eli, or Elmer, or Ralph. And then I remembered what year it was. Well, maybe grandkids. The small group wandered down from the church steps and out into the sun and gathered in front of the video store next door. A video store. Crum had changed some, after all.

I had been in Crum for less than two hours, but I had done what I set out to do. I had gone back to Crum, and I had found no more nightmares buried in my mind. It was still Crum. But I was not me.

I had seen no one I knew. I didn't really expect to. After all, what did I really expect after all this time? Nothing much. And what would I say to them if I did see them?

One or two of the men in the restaurant had gone, and one or two had taken their places. They paid little attention to me, content to talk to each other and to the ladies behind the counter. I was an outsider. Just passing through. Didn't really belong there.

One of the men had been there when I came in, and he was there still. Tall, angular, with a face that was both sad and intelligent, he sat at a front table, at ease with the other men, but saying little. Gathering, I thought. He's gathering. I did that myself, sometimes, just sat and watched and gathered and stored. Collecting stories, I would say to myself. Stories just don't happen, they have to be taken in. And this guy is doing the same. He's gathering.

And he was the only one in the place who paid any attention that I was there. I noticed it when I first came in. He stared, then looked away, then stared again. After all, I was an outsider. I didn't belong in Crum. And isn't that the point of the whole thing — that I had *never* belonged in Crum? At least one of them should be able to stare if he wanted.

It was time to go. I walked to the cash register beside the door and paid for the coffee. Before I could pocket the change he was standing beside me, inches taller than I, imposing.

"You used to live in Crum?" he asked, his voice soft with West Virginia accent.

"Yes. But a long time ago."

"You used to live behind that house there?" He pointed across the tracks at Bascomb's old house.

All I could do was nod.

"Howdy, Lee, old friend," he said, extending his hand. "My name's David Varney."